Robert C Scott

Trials of Scott and Dunlap

Robbing the Northampton National Bank and Breaking and Entering the

Cashier's House

Robert C Scott

Trials of Scott and Dunlap
Robbing the Northampton National Bank and Breaking and Entering the Cashier's House

ISBN/EAN: 9783337815905

Printed in Europe, USA, Canada, Australia, Japan

Cover: Foto ©Andreas Hilbeck / pixelio.de

More available books at **www.hansebooks.com**

An Astounding Record of Crime and its Exposure.

TRIALS OF SCOTT AND DUNLAP

FOR

Robbing the Northampton National Bank,

AND.

Breaking and Entering the Cashier's House.

Twelve Days in Court.

VERBATIM REPORTS OF THE ADDRESSES TO THE JURY, BY

Hon. EDWARD B. GILLETT, of Westfield,
Hon. N. A. LEONARD, of Springfield, and
H. H. BOND, Esq, of Northampton.

Sketch of Bank Burglaries Planned and Executed by Edson, Scott, Dunlap,
Connors, and others.—Nearly $3,000,000 Stolen.

Pinkerton's National Detective Agency.

ALLAN PINKERTON, Principal.   GEO. H. BANGS, Gen. Sup't.
CLARENCE A. SEWARD, Counsel and Attorney, 29 Nassau St., N. Y.

OFFICES.

NEW YORK—66 Exchange Place, Rob't A. Pinkerton, Sup't.
CHICAGO—191 & 193 Fifth Avenue, - F. Warner, Sup't.
PHILADELPHIA—45 S. Third St., Benj. Franklin, Sup't.

☞ This Agency does not operate for contingent rewards ; is independent of Government or Municipal control, and prepared to do all legitimate Detective business entrusted to it by Express, Railroad or Insurance Companies, and Banks or Individuals.

The Great Bank Burglary.

Trial of Scott and Dunlap for Robbing the Northampton National Bank.

On the night of Tuesday, January 25, 1876, seven masked men entered, simultaneously, the house of John Whittelsey, cashier of the Northampton National Bank, captured the seven inmates of the house, bound and gagged them, and by force and torture obtained from the cashier the combination to the lock on the door of the bank vault. They also took from the cashier his gold watch. Then, repairing to the bank, they entered the front door with the key taken from the cashier, and by means of the combinations obtained from him, opened the vault, and took therefrom money, bonds, certificates, and other securities of the face value of about one and a quarter millions of dollars. Of that amount, $111,250 was the property of the bank, and the balance was the property of private depositors. The burglars locked the vault door when they left, and wrenched off the dial. An expert locksmith from New York was sent for to unlock the vault door, and it was not until about twenty hours after the robbery that the fact of the robbery was definitely known. The robbery was committed between the hours of four and six o'clock on the morning of the 26th, and the robbers left town immediately thereafter.

On February 14, 1877, Robert Scott and James Dunlap, well known to the police force of New York as professional bank robbers, were arrested in Philadelphia, as the ringleaders in this robbery, and on the 17th of that month were brought to Northampton and committed to the county jail. On the 22d and 23d of March, they were examined in the Town Hall, before Trial Justice H. H. Chilson, and bound over for trial in the Superior Court, in June, under bonds of $500,000 each. Since that time, they have remained in jail here, under a constant special guard, both inside and outside of the jail premises.

At the session of the Grand Jury, June 12, Scott and Dunlap were indicted for breaking and entering Cashier Whittelsey's house and stealing his gold watch, and also for breaking and entering the bank, and stealing money and securities therefrom. When the case was called, in the Superior Court, on the 19th of June, a postponement was secured until Monday, July 9, at 2 o'clock P. M., when the trial was commenced before Judge John W. Bacon, of Natick, one of the Justices of the Superior Court.

To both of the indictments, the prisoners, when arraigned on June 15, pleaded not guilty. The government first took up the indictment charging the offence of breaking and entering the bank and stealing therefrom.

The Indictment.

COMMONWEALTH OF MASSACHUSETTS.

HAMPSHIRE SS.—At the Superior Court begun and holden at Northampton within and for the County of Hampshire, on the 2d Monday of June, 1877.

The Jurors for said Commonwealth on their oath present, that Robert Scott and James Dunlap, both of the State of New York, on the 26th day of January, 1876, at Northampton, in said county of Hampshire and Commonwealth of Massachusetts aforesaid, with force and arms a certain building there situate, to wit, the banking-house of the Northampton National Bank, of Northampton, a corporation there established by law, in the night time of said day did break and enter with intent then and there the goods, chattels and moneys of the Northampton National Bank, of Northampton aforesaid, feloniously to steal, take and carry away, and sundry legal tender notes issued by the United States of America for the payment of moneys, together amounting to six thousand dollars, and of the value of six thousand dollars; sundry National Bank notes for the payment of moneys, together amounting to six thousand dollars, and of the value of six thousand dollars; seventy-five mortgage bonds issued by the Ohio and Mississippi Railroad Company, each for the payment of one thousand dollars, and each of the value of one thousand dollars; five bonds issued by the State of Missouri, each for the payment of one thousand dollars, and each of the value of one thousand dollars, of the goods, chattels and moneys of the Northampton National Bank of Northampton aforesaid, then and there in the building aforesaid being found, feloniously did steal, take and carry away, against the peace of said Commonwealth and contrary to the form of the statute in such case made and provided.

A true bill.   H. C. M. HOWE, Foreman.
S. T. FIELD, District Attorney.

Opening of the Court.

Promptly on time, (2 o'clock Monday afternoon,) the Judge arrived and the court was opened. A few minutes previous, the prisoners were brought in. Scott was handcuffed to Deputy Sheriff Potter, and Dunlap was handcuffed to Deputy Sheriff Munyan. The The prisoners looked in good physical condition. Dunlap especially seems to have improved since he entered upon his confinement. The High Sheriff, H. A. Longley, and ten deputies were in attendance.

Mr. Gillett Admitted to Assist the District Attorney.

District Attorney Field asked the court to be allowed to call to his assistance Edward B. Gillett, of Westfield. Mr. Sweetser, counsel for the defendants objected. The Judge said he should allow Mr. Gillett to assist the District Attorney, if he (Gillett) should say that he was not to be paid by any outside party. Mr. Gillett stated to the court that he had not been retained by any party in this case for pay; that he had no expectation of receiving pay, and that he was here without bias, and with no hope of compensation. In reply to questions by Mr. Sweetser, Mr. Gillett said he was first invited to assist in this case by Charles Delano, of Northampton, by letter, who wrote at the request of the Dist. Attorney, and afterward by Dist. Attorney Field, in a letter. Mr. Sweetser asked if he should assist, and shouldn't receive some present from the bank, whether he would not consider it a pretty mean bank. Mr. Gillett said he should not care to have his virtue tested in that way, and would answer when he answered the letter containing the offer. Mr. Sweetser inquired if Mr. Gillett was to be allowed to make the final argument, and the Judge replied that he could do whatever the District Attorney asked him to do. While the management and responsible control of the case was, and would continue to be, in the hands of the District Attorney, he could direct what part of the duties of conducting the case Mr. Gillett should perform. Mr. Sweetser desired to put in an exception to this ruling.

The Counsel.

The prosecution, being a duty assumed by the government, was in the hands of the District Attorney, who was the only prosecuting officer known to the law in the case. He was assisted by Mr. Gillett, who made the final argument. Charles Delano and Geo. M. Stearns sat near the prosecuting counsel, to make such suggestions as their familiarity with the case dictated. The defense was conducted by Theo. H. Sweetser, of Boston, and D. W. & H. H. Bond of this town. J. M. Moore, of New York, a friend of Scott, who has been working up the case in New York, procuring evidence of alibies, &c., was also present to aid in the defense, and Detective Pinkerton of N. Y. was present to aid the prosecution.

The Jury.

About an hour was consumed in impannelling the jury. The government challenged two jurors and the defense two, and four had formed an opinion. The jury having been filled, the Judge stated that he should allow the jury to appoint their own foreman when they retired to consider upon their verdict.

The Jury.—Calvin Pease, Belchertown ; A. D. Perry, Worthington ; Norman Preston, South Hadley ; Horace Rhoades, Chesterfield ; E. Sheldon Searle, Southampton ; Frederick C. Shaw, Easthampton ; Geo. Tower, Westhampton ; Thomas W. Stratton, Pelham ; Fred D. Billings, Hatfield ; Alfred H. Cook, Hadley ; Joshua Crosby, Williamsburg ; Jesse L. Gale, Easthampton.

Opening the Case.

District Attorney Field opened the case for the prosecution, giving a summary of what the government expected to prove. It would offer testimony to prove that this robbery was committed, and that it was committed by these defendants. It would offer the testimony of a man who was one of the parties concerned in the robbery prior to its commission. It proposed to show that this witness (Edson) who was in collusion with these defendants to rob the Northampton Bank, was also in collusion with them to rob a bank in Elmira, N. Y. He had now turned state's evidence, and was willing to testify to what he knew, and having been with these defendants, aiding and abetting them, he knew all about their operations. The law wisely availed itself of the evidence of one guilty party to convict other guilty ones.

The Evidence.

The first witness called was Engineer *E. C. Davis*, of Northampton, who exhibited a plan of Cashier Whittelsey's house on Elm street, made by him. The house is distant from the bank 230¼ rods, or about two-thirds of a mile.

The next witness was *John Whittelsey*, Cashier of the Northampton Bank, who told the story of the visit of the robbers to his house on the night of January 25, 1876. They entered a little after midnight ; saw five of them, all wearing masks ; one went to his bedside and handcuffed him; another to the other side of the bed and handcuffed his wife. These two men he identified as the defendants Scott and Dunlap. All the inmates of the house, seven in number, were gathered in his bedroom, and afterward five of them were taken into other rooms, and confined by lashing them to the bedsteads. Mr. Whittelsey was ordered to dress, and was assisted in dressing by Scott, and soon was taken into the hall adjoining his bedroom, where he was guarded in turn by both Scott and Dunlap. He told them it was no use for them to attempt to get into the bank, as it was secured by locks that were regarded as safe. One of them replied they knew more about locks than he did. They said they were going to take him to the bank and make him open the vault, and if didn't do it they would "make it hot for him." He was then taken down stairs, and the bank keys demanded. One of the robbers took a key from his own pocket, and asked if that was the key to the bank door. Whittelsey told them it was ; it was a key which one of the robbers had taken from his pantaloons pocket. The robber tried the key in the lock to the front door to the house which it fitted. He then accused Whittelsey of lying to him. This man was Scott. Dunlap asked me if I wanted some brandy—was not feeling well. Told him no ; I was better. When down stairs, Scott was behind or beside me, and Dunlap near. Scott asked if I was not at Watch Hill two years before, in the Summer. Told him I was there. Said he was there also. Asked Dunlap to close the kitchen door. He, replied it was well enough as it was. Scott called for the combination of the lock on the vault. I gave him incorrect figues. He took them down and asked for the combination on the inner door. That door was not locked. Scott said he would not believe it. Gave him figures. He asked for the combination on the inside safe. When I hesitated, he struck me with a sharp pointed pencil. Asked me to repeat the figures. Tried to do so, but couldn't remember the figures I had given him. One of them said it was no use for me to lie to them, and began pounding, choking and punching me. Dunlap was behind me, with a pistol, and Scott before me. Scott took the number. I watched him closely. They then blindfolded me. They were in the house three hours. Scott assisted me to dress—went with me to the closet—asked if I had but one vest. Dunlap sat beside me at least two hours. They were there from soon after 12 to 4. After I gave them the correct combination, they were satisfied they had obtained it. I was led to a bedroom, and there gagged and bound to the bed. Dunlap said bind this man close, so he can't get away. That was about 4. It was about half past 3 when went down stairs. The first of the robbers to leave the house were Scott and Dunlap. It was nearly 6 when the last two of them left. I was released between 6 and 7. Seven persons in the house—myself and wife, Miss Mattie White (now Mrs. Page,) Mr. and Mrs. F. B. Cutler, Miss Benton, and a servant girl. Mrs. Whittelsey appealed to one of the robbers to treat her husband kindly. Heard her ask him if he was a married man, to which he replied that he was. Robber said he would treat Mr. Whittelsey well, if he would do as they wanted to have him. Reached the bank at 7—found the vault door locked, and dial broken off. A man came from New York to unlock the vault. Opened it the night after the robbery. There were stolen of the bank's property, $12,000 in bank bills, $6,000 in government notes, five $1,000 bonds of the State of Missouri, and $75,000 of Ohio and Mississippi R. R. bonds, of the market value of $850 per $1,000 of face value, and a large number of notes, all the property of the bank.

At this point, it was five o'clock, and the Judge said he would adjourn the court until Tuesday morning, at 9. The hours of meeting during the trial were fixed at 9 A. M. and 2.15 P. M., and of adjourning, 12.45 and 5.15 P. M. The Judge cautioned the jury against allowing any person to talk about the trial in their presence, or to them about it, or to talk among themselves about it, but to keep themselves free from bias, so to render an unbiased and impartial verdict.

At about 4 o'clock, a heavy shower came on, and the noise of the pouring rain almost drowned the proceedings in the court room. Darkness prevailed to such an extent that for about half an hour it was necessary to light the gas.

Tuesday Morning.

Cashier Whittelsey, resumed. Aggregate amount taken from the bank estimated at from $1,000,000 to $1,250,000. Much of it belonged to private parties, some of whom lost their all. (Judge ruled that all the government was obliged to prove was the breaking and entering the bank.) I had one of the three keys necessary to open the vault. These keys had been repaired ; in fall of 1875 were filed. District Attorney asked who did the filing? Sweetser objected. Judge admitted the evidence. In fall of 1875, the keys were placed in hands of Wm. D. Edson to be filed. He took them into the directors' room and filed them. Had seen Edson before. Found three of the doors at house broken morning after robbery; broken with sledge hammers—found five such hammers in house. Also found other tools in house—gimlets, &c. My watch and chain were taken by Scott. Scott had the watch down stairs. Asked him not to take it away ; said he would not. Watch and chain valued at $250. The robbers wore masks. The two men with me in the house were Scott and Dunlap. "I have no hesitation in saying they were the two men on trial." Identify them by their voice, size and shape. Their voices impressed me more than anything else. The men were addressed by numbers. Taller man was Scott ; he was addressed as No. 1. Judged him to be the leader of the gang. He demanded of me the combination. Can't say who gave directions to the others. Their voices impressed me. Suspected they might be arrested some time, and watched them closely. First heard them speak since the robbery, February 27, 1877, and for three days in succession. Noticed particularly Scott's broad shoulders.

(Here the sledge hammers found in the house were shown. The doors bore marks of blows with such hammers. Other articles were exhibited—dark lanterns, masks, hooks, gimlets, straps, cords, rubbers, dusters.)

Cross-examined by Mr. Sweetser. Scott wore a long linen duster, buttoned, coming nearly to his knees. Wore a mask. Could not see his face. He wore gloves. Saw his general form. Didn't notice his feet. He wore rubbers. Dunlap wore darker clothes—wore a jacket and overalls. Identified the mask he wore, but afterward said he could not positively say that any particular man wore a particular one of these articles. Asked if there was anything extraordinary about Scott. Said he was broad-shouldered. Here Sweetser asked Scott to stand up, and he did so; also Dunlap. Is there anything about these men extraordinary ? Witness said there was not, but he could readily distinguish their forms. Was excited that night—frightened—for a time, but afterward got over it. Was blindfolded when tied to the bed. Heard the doors close. Three men left the house at about 4. Did not see them when they left, but heard their steps. Did not see the men on trial for more than a year. First saw them in the jail, in the chapel. Went there to see the prisoners. Prior to going to the jail had heard something of the evidence against these men. Heard it from the officers of the bank. Had not heard it from any detective. Saw Pinkerton prior to going to the jail—at the bank, on Sunday morning. Am in the habit of visiting the bank Sunday mornings. No talk at that time with regard to the evidence against these men. Think there was talk at that time of my going to the jail to see these men. Heard some of the evidence before the men were arrested. Heard Scott say "yes" at the jail—heard Dunlap say the same. Did not tell anybody I recognized their voices. Saw them the next day, at jail. Mrs. Whittelsey and Miss White were there also. Conversed about the matter between these two days. Officers of the bank wanted me to go there. Scott asked Pinkerton, "Have you seen my wife lately ?" and said, "I would like what money was found on me ;" also, "If I had my own way." Heard Dunlap say, "Will you see about my trunk and have it left in Mrs. Scott's care ?" He asked, "How is Connors' case getting on ?" Heard them the next day, at the jail. Told officers of the bank thought I recognized these men.

Scott asked what he was to have for breakfast—said it was fish day. Said it was useless to canonize saints, as some of them died of small pox. Recognize them by something besides the voice. A peculiar shrug of the shoulders. Recognize Scott by his shrug. Saw it at the jail, where he exhibited the shrug several times. Sweetser asked, for the purpose of testing witness' mind as to his entire fairness, and wanted him to be cautious in answering : If having no other evidence than the shrug of his shoulders, he could swear that Scott was the man who broke into witness' house ? Witness said no. Sweetser then asked, if there was no other evidence than his recognition of the voice, he could swear that this man was guilty ? Witness said yes, and repeated it two or three times. Scott here stood up and, at Sweetser's request, spoke several words. Witness said he suppressed his voice. Mr. Gillett objected to Scott's talking in this way for this purpose. The Judge ruled out this mode of examination. Defense noted the exception. Some hair was taken out of one of the masks by Mr. Hussey, and has been carefully kept at the bank.

The next witness was *E. A. Hall*, of the firm of Hall & Prew, Springfield, dealers in clothing, who testified that a pair of the overalls found at Whittelsey's house, and a pair of drawers and socks, were purchased at his store in January, 1876, a day or two prior to the robbery, but could not tell who bought them. His cross-examination postponed.

James O. Mantor, a workman at the hoe factory, early in January, 1876, saw on two different evenings, two men standing in front of Cashier Whittelsey's house, talking and making gestures. His impression was that Scott was one of those men, but he could not say positively.

David W. Crafts saw on Elm street, in January, 1876, a man who inquired of him where Whittelsey lived. Feel satisfied that the man I saw was Scott. Prior to Jan. 25, 1876, saw in front of Maynard & Brooks' store, a man whom he called the same man he saw on Elm street. Defense declined to cross-examine the witness.

Deputy Sheriff *Ansel Wright* testified to finding in the attic of the Bridge street school-house, a day previous to the robbery, a lot of blankets, cold chicken and bread in a mouldy state. Blankets were rolled up. A paper bag found there bore the printed card of the N. Y. & N. H. R. R. Stamford Restaurant. No cross-examination.

Deputy Sheriff *Henry M. Potter* found the goods in the school-house attic. Found there a copy of the N. Y. Sun, dated Dec. 22, 1875.

Deputy Sheriff Wright, recalled, testified to finding a flask of whiskey, in the school-house attic, with the label of a N. Y. firm upon it.

Edson on the Stand.

At a quarter before twelve o'clock, *Wm. D. Edson* was called and sworn. Residence in New York. Resided there since June, 1871. Knew Scott and Dunlap since September, 1873. My business was making sales of safes for Herring & Co. During fall of 1873, met Scott and Dunlap four or five times previous to an attempted robbery. Met him at Wm. Connors' room on Houston street, N. Y., in 1873. Sweetser objected to witness testifying as to a robbery in the fall of 1873, as it had nothing to do with the robbery of the Northampton Bank. District Attorney Field claimed it as competent, as part of a conspiracy, resulting in the robbery of this bank. Mr. Gillett claimed that, as early as 1873, a compact was entered into between Edson, Connors, Scott and Dunlap for robbing banks—that each of the conspirators was to keep on the watch for banks that could be successfully robbed, and that when such a bank was found, it was to be attacked ; and that, in pursuance of that conspiracy, the Northampton bank was robbed. Mr. Sweetser objected, because whatever was said about robbing banks at that time had nothing to do with the robbery of the Northampton bank. The court allowed the evidence of conspiracy to be admitted, and counsel for defense gave notice of exception.

Edson's Testimony.

Edson testified. Met Scott in Elmira, N. Y., in September, 1875. I was sitting at the dinner table on Sunday, when a stranger came to me after all the guests had left, and gave me a letter from a gentleman whom I met soon afterwards in my room, and who introduced himself as Robert Scott. He was registered at the hotel as Fisher, of Illinois. He gave me a letter from one Wm. Connors. There was an arrangement made to rob banks by Scott, Dunlap and myself, at my house in 1873 ; there were present Scott, Dunlap and Connors. Scott asked me for the use of an air pump which I had, and which was used for the sole purpose of breaking into banks, and under the consideration that if their arrangements should succeed they were to give me an equal share in any bank they robbed. I asked them if such arrangements would be satisfactory in every way, and they said they would. In pursuance of that conversation, I gave them an air pump with that understanding. I did not see anything more of either of them for, probably, in the neighborhood of a month. Then I think I saw Scott. He said he received a dispatch from Dunlap asking him to make preparations to go west. At the time the arrangement was made I was to give them all the information I could. I had an opportunity of going where they could not. In pursuance of this agreement I was to receive an equal division of the property.

I came to Northampton to look at their banks, and report to the defendants at Wilkes-barre, Pa.   I came in August, and had an arrangement in case I was detained.   I could telegraph them, Care of R. C. Hill, Wyoming House, Wilkesbarre, Pa.   I came to North-ampton on some work for the First National Bank and was detained, and telegraphed to Wilkesbarre that I would meet them at R. L. Edwards', 241 West Second street, N. Y. After I finished my business I went to New York and from there to Wilkesbarre, in re-sponse to a telegram, and met Scott and Dunlap.   I gave them the information I had about the dial, and explained that the lock had a weakness in it which rendered it unfit for use.   I had with me a set of keys which Mr. Warriner had given me.   I gave them to Mr. Scott and we came to New York together.   I also gave him keys to a sample dial. He made a set of duplicates and came to my home, and returned the set belonging to the bank.   Mr. Dunlap was with him and they practiced working the dial.   I think they then agreed to go to Northampton in a day or two, which they did.   That I know.   They told me they had been here, and found where Mr. Whittelsey lived, what part of the house, how many were in his family, etc.   Afterwards there was another meeting, when Connors was also present and all three agreed to go, and afterwards I saw them again and they said they had been to Northampton.   They said they had watched Whittelsey's movements and those of the watchmen of the bank and of the town, and saw that in order to be successful they must take care of all the watchmen in the town.   I told Scott and Dunlap that Locke, an employe of Herring & Co., had received a letter from the bank in Northampton, stating that their dials were worthless, and told them they had better drop the job.   At their request I went on to Northampton and saw Mr. Edwards and Mr. Warriner, and found that the dials were out of order, and went back and told them that they had better stop work then, and nothing was done in September and until November.   They then went to Northampton and examined the First National Bank, and came back and reported they had found obstructions which they wanted me to advise them about.   (This was objected to by Mr. Sweetser and ruled out by the court as referr-ing to a bank other than the one robbed.)

Afterwards Scott, Dunlap and Connors wanted me to come on and see about the North-ampton National Bank, and I did, on the 22d of November, and obtained impressions of the keys at the bank, and told them I had obtained the impressions and gave them to him, and that while fixing the lock on the second door of the safe, I suggested to Mr. Warriner to look at the outer door, and did take off the lock, and also that of the safe door.   I suggested that it wasn't safe for a young man to know the combination, and it was changed, and only Mr. Whittelsey and one other knew it.   I did not find out the combi-nation then, but did afterwards, and gave it to the defendants.   I knew then that Mr. Whittelsey had it, and that he could also open the other doors, and if he could not, I could do a little.

Tuesday Afternoon.

I gave the impressions which I took here on the 24th of November to Scott and Dun-lap : I met them about the 26th ; I think we were to see them again early in the follow-ing week ; I think they came to my house then and showed the keys Scott had made, and tried the dials of the locks.   I had five or six interviews with them until January, when the robbery occurred.   At one of these they told me that after one of their visits here they were out of funds, and wanted me to raise some money, and I told them I thought I could, provided the terms were satisfactory for its use ; five per cent. on the proceeds of the robbery were the terms, but it was not satisfactory.   Finally I got $1000 for them, they to pay $10,000 for the use of it.   They came here early in January, I think, with the purpose of perpetrating the robbery, but came back without doing it. and without money.   I raised them $300 more and gave it to them.   I met Dunlap on Broadway the Sunday night preceding the robbery, and he told me they were going to Northampton the next day.   The Monday evening following the 26th of January, I saw Dunlap and Scott. I was here at the opening of the vault : I was sent here from Bristol, Conn.   I was in New York on the morning of the robbery.   When I got here I found another workman from Herring & Co.'s was expected here.   When he came he opened the vault by attach-ing a dial to the spindle, which was exposed, with one hundred numbers, and of course the combination would be struck with that number of numbers.   When the safe was opened, Messrs. Edwards and Warriner were present, and we found an empty safe, a safe not opened, and also a pocket-book which had not been taken.   I next met Scott and

Dunlap in response to a personal in the New York Herald we had agreed upon if they wanted to see me ; we met on the Monday following the robbery. (Copy of Herald shown witness.) That is the Herald and the personal. The personal meant I was to meet Mr. Connors at the corner of 34th street and Broadway at 8 o'clock Monday evening. I put in a personal myself, but met Mr. Conners, and he took me to 60th street and 10th avenue and met Scott, and afterwards Dunlap. Conners at this time handed me a portion of the money taken from the safe ; I think about $1200. I asked them who took that watch ? I said it was a small piece of business. Scott said it was a mistake, and would be returned. I asked them if they had any trouble, and Dunlap said "no." I asked them if they abused Mr. Whittelsey, and they said no ; they struck him once in the breast. I had several interviews with them, and during one of them Dunlap spoke of Mrs. Whittelsey being a very courageous woman, and of her stroking Dunlap's hand when they were tying her husband, and begging them not to hurt him. I met Dunlap about the middle of the week, near 50th street and 5th avenue, and at that interview the subject of conversation was the search for the securities by detectives. I asked him if Scott had returned them, and he said no. I told him there was a strong probability of the securities being found, and they had better settle, and they could do so safely. I also tried Dunlap. I had put a personal in the Herald to recall Scott from coming here after the securities. It read: "Knox, come home." Conners told me he would know what it meant, as he (Scott) formerly had a horse by that name. At one of these interviews I asked Scott and Dunlap whether they hurt any of these parties, and they said they frightened a servant girl. They complained that I had not told them right in regard to a key of the bank door. I explained how they were wrong, and they said they thought Mr. Whittelsey was lying to them, because he insisted it was the key of the bank. I made an arrangement to meet them Sunday night, the 13th of February, in New York, and they came about 10 o'clock in a carriage. I proposed to them to allow the property to be found at Northampton. They wanted to know the terms, and I told them I didn't know. I also explained to them how it could be done. I finally left them with an understanding that they were ready to negotiate. I asked Dunlap if Scott had returned, and he said no. I know I afterwards met Scott, and he told me he had been in Springfield. When I first saw them after the robbery, they said they had taken out $900 for the purpose of buying a team to drive up here and get the securities.

At the interview, February 13, I talked with Scott about his journey to Springfield, and he said they went up from New Haven in a sleigh, drove to Hartford where they exchanged their sleigh for a buggy. At Springfield they read an account of the search for the bonds, and returned to New York.

My next interview with them was on the Wednesday evening following. I met only Scott, on the corner of 34th street and Madison avenue, and walked to a beer saloon between Third street and Lexington avenue. He asked if I had been to Northampton and I said yes ; he asked me what they were willing to give for the return of the securities and I told him about $60,000 ; he asked me to get from the bank a list of the value of the securities, which I did, I think, from Mr. Williams. I showed it to him afterwards and while doing so he seemed to be pre-occupied, and after looking a while he gave me to understand that they were not willing to negotiate on the bank's terms, and told me Dunlap and another had gone up here to get them. He evidently was suspicious of me. I met him Friday evening next at a lager beer saloon ; he placed himself where he could see the entrance to the saloon. I asked him if Dunlap had returned and he said "yes," but he was sick, having broke into Mill river when coming back. He said the securities were in New York, and he wanted me to go down and see them. He made an appointment two nights afterwards, which I kept, but never saw him then nor afterwards until the following September, when I saw him in University Park, and asked him if he was not going to settle the matter and give me a share of the securities, and he said "not a d——d cent." I asked him why, and he said that I had given the whole party away. I denied it and tried to induce them to settle. During the interview, I asked him if he was certain I had given the party away, and he said no, as I could not have been selling them. I never saw him again until the 9th of November, when I met Mr. Scott, who told me those men wanted to see me. I told him I wanted to speak to my family, and he finally consented. We went finally on the outskirts of Prospect Park, where I met both Scott and Dunlap. We talked over the division. I asked if all the party would be satisfied with a division which would give each his fair portion, and Scott said they would have to do so. I told them everything I knew, and Scott said I told them nothing they did not know, while Dunlap said it was "all n d——d lie," and he didn't believe a word of it. Dunlap wanted to know what the Northampton people would give to let him go. I told him I didn't know ; I thought $100,000, or, perhaps $150,000 ; he said if they would do that they could have their securities. I told them they could arrange an interview with the bank people, but they said the bank people knew where to find them if they wanted them. I told them they had better settle very soon, as they were well known by others, and were in danger, for up to that time, the 9th of November, I had not opened my lips about them to a living man. The Sunday following I met Scott at "Red" Leary's, near Hamilton Ferry, in New York. I told them I had seen Mr. Williams, and they could settle it. He threatened me at that time if there was trouble, as I told him there would surely be. I left him with the promise from him that he would see Mr. Williams. He said he was not afraid to get arrested and always carried a thousand dollars to ventilate old Herring, if they were arrested. The name of the third man at the Prospect Park interview was John Leary. Mr. Connors was to have the negotiation of the division of the plunder and I took Mr. Williams to Connors at 616 Broadway ; (exceptions taken ;) I think it was Wednesday evening, November 15 ; (exceptions taken.) Have known Scott under the names of Robert Bush and Mitchell, and Dunlap under the names of Horace C. Hill and Borden.

Edson Cross-examined by Mr. Sweetser.

Have been employed by Herring since June, 1872, to January, 1877, when I resigned. Was in the harness business in Minneapolis, Minnesota, three years prior ; was in N. Y. three months prior, and in Montreal, Canada ; previous to that in Philadelphia ; had some trouble when I left Boston ; I was arrested in Boston at the instance of a woman, who tried to black mail me ; the first bank I was concerned in attempting to rob was the First National Bank of Elmira ; the second was the bank in Quincy, Ill. ; the attempt at Elmira was in 1873, and at Saratoga in 1874, and the Long Island National in the winter of 1874 and 1875 ; the next was at Covington, Ky., in March, 1875, and the bank at Rockville, Conn., in 1875, and at Pittston, Pa., November, 1875, and Northampton National, Jan. 26, 1876. There was an attempt at Wilkesbarre, Pa., and at Nantucket, I think, in the summer of 1873, and the Third National Bank of Syracuse in June, 1875. I got out of the Bank of Illinois $7,600 ; out of the Pittston $850. Never had a quarrel with Scott and Dunlap before the Northampton bank robbery. Had hard feelings against them in April, 1874, when they robbed and beat me.

I superintended putting in the doors of the Northampton bank for Herring & Co., in 1874. I might have arranged it so that a visit to the Cashier would not have been necessary. I told the story which I have, for self-interest and self-protection. Firstmentioned that I was a party to the crime in November, 1876. I considered that the parties concerned in the robbery had not treated me fairly, and I wanted to have them restore the money to parties who needed it. I first had an intimation that it was known I was connected with the Northampton bank robbery from John Kenney, a professional thief in New York, who said there was not an old knuck-moll in New York who didn't know all about it. I was offered from $10,000 to $25,000, by Mr. Edwards of the bank, to make a clean breast of it. I was influenced to do so by the fact that I had given my word to Mr. Williams that he should have the property back.

At an interview with Mr. Williams at the 5th Avenue Hotel, I told him that if he would guarantee $100,000 and give me my own way, I would try and get the property back.

Wednesday—Third Day.

EXCITING SCENE IN THE COURT ROOM—MR. SWEETSER ABRUPTLY WITHDRAWS FROM THE CASE.

At the opening of the court on Wednesday morning, Mr. Gillett stated that the government desired to withdraw so much of the evidence of the witness Edson, given on Tuesday, as related to what was said concerning the visit of Connors to Springfield. At the time these statements were testified to, Mr. Sweetser objected and gave notice of exceptions, whereupon the District Attorney withdrew them. Mr. Sweetser claimed at the time that they could not be withdrawn after having been made in the presence of the jury, without leaving more or less of effect prejudicial to the defendants upon the minds of the jurors. The Judge then ruled them all out, and stated that he should so instruct the jury.

Immediately after Mr. Gillett had moved to have Connors' statements ruled out, on Wednesday morning, Mr. Sweetser said that if matters were to be placed before the jury, which leave an impression upon the minds of the jury, which even the instructions of the court could not remove, and which the defense could not remove by evidence, "I shall retire from this court house, for I can no longer benefit these defendants, if such a course is pursued."

The Judge said he remembered that his ruling was in accordance with what he had stated, and he should now rule as he ruled then. "I shall rule all evidence out in regard to Connors' statements, when the defendants were not present."

At this point, Mr. Sweetser picked up his hat and left the court-room, proceeding to the Mansion House. Edson was then on the stand, awaiting the continuance of the cross-examination. The court-room was crowded, every available place being occupied. The scene was intensely exciting. It was dramatic. Everyone instinctively asked, What does this mean? Is it for effect? or, Is it an honest abandonment of the case for cause deemed sufficient? The Bond Brothers seemed to be as much surprised by the action of Sweetser as any of the audience; and apparently the prisoners were surprised. They appeared agitated, nervous. The Bond Brothers counseled together a few minutes, and conferred with the prisoners. Then they asked of the court a delay of a few minutes that they might go out and consult Mr. Sweetser.

The Judge replied that he did not know that he was called upon to allow delay for consultation with Mr. Sweetser. "He is out of the case by his own statement, and has withdrawn from it, for effect, as I believe."

Mr. Bond said he hardly thought His Honor was justified in making that statement.

The Judge replied—I know what I ruled yesterday, and Mr. Sweetser attempted to have me rule otherwise to-day. *When it is threatened that counsel will withdraw from the case unless I back down, then I don't back down.* This announcement, given in a calm, yet very firm and decided manner, was greeted with a rustle of suppressed applause, and had it not been for the restraint of the court-room, the outburst of approval would have been universal and uproarious.

The Judge again said he should instruct the jury to strike out all evidence of Connors relating to the case.

Mr. Bond said he did not think the prisoners should suffer because Mr. Sweetser had had a little misunderstanding with the court. Mr. Sweetser believed the court had done wrong, and he (Bond) believed Sweetser was honest in saying what he had said.

The Judge decided to allow a reasonable time for consultation, and Mr. H. H. Bond left the court-room and went to the Mansion House, where he found Mr. Sweetser and had a conference with him; after which he returned to the court-room, and announced to the court that they would go on with the case.

Mr. D. W. Bond then took up the cross-examination of Edson, who testified as follows :—My wife is living. Have only one wife. Was married in 1865. Had nothing to do with an attempt to rob the Sixth Avenue bank at New York, in the summer of 1876 —furnished no plans, pencil work, drawings or cards. Scott and Dunlap stated to me that they entered the bank, alone. Here the cross-examination stopped.

The next witness was Albert Holt, paymaster of the Boston and Albany railroad company. On January 25, 1876, at about 8 A. M. he saw two men crossing Main street, Springfield, from Cooley's hotel. Was in front of them. Afterwards saw the same men come out of the depot and pass down the street, where they met three other men, with whom they talked a minute, and then separated. In the afternoon, saw the two turn down Pynchon street, where they again met the three men, with whom they had a conversation and separated. Saw the two men the next morning enter a store on Main street. Have no doubt about either day. They were strangers. One was taller than the other; had a dark complexion and a small moustache. The other had light hair and a moustache. Saw the same men at the examination of this case. I see them here, (pointing to Scott and Dunlap.) Been paymaster of the B. and A. road 19 years.

Cross-examined. Saw the two men a few minutes on January 25. One wore his hair long, and a silk hat.

Benjamin Franklin, one of Pinkerton's detectives, saw the defendants February 11,

1877, at the depot in Philadelphia. They were on the express train going South. Had a warrant for their arrest. Took them off the train. They had a package with them. District Attorney desired to prove that this package contained burglars' tools like those found in Whittelsey's house, but court ruled that he could not. Their tickets were for Richmond, Va. Witness identified the handwriting of Scott and Dunlap. Showed them the warrant when they were arrested. Told them my name and business. They said I was mistaken. Scott would not admit his identity and would not sign the order for the return of his money. They made no admissions. Witness was not cross-examined.

Mrs. Whittelsey. The first thing I heard, a man came into the room, and I heard screaming through the house, and then a tall man came into the room where we were, and then Mr. Whittelsey and Mrs. Page and myself were requested to get up and dress, which request we obeyed. I assisted Mr. Whittelsey to dress, and it seemed to annoy the tall man who seemed to give the orders, and he requested me to go over to the other side of the room, and I did so. By the light of a dark lantern which they carried, I could well see their movements. They opened all the bureau drawers and scattered the contents over the floor, and the tall man requested one attendant to look after them. My attendant requested Mrs. Page and myself to be seated, and we were, and he seated himself beside us. We sat there some time, about half an hour. I requested him to treat Mr. Whittelsey kindly, and he said he would, if he did as they requested him. I asked him if he had a wife. He replied that he had. I then asked him if he had any children, and he said yes. I asked him how old they were, and he said not very old, and then he told me we could go into another room. One of the party had on a black cap, and they wore masks. We were liberated about 6.30 A. M. I think we were in our room until 1 o'clock. They spoke to each other. I counted five as the dark lanterns' light came together. They addressed each other. I heard numbers called, and supposed they were known by numbers. The tall one gave the orders. He was very nervous in manner all the evening, and manifested it by shrugging his shoulders, and in other ways. The attendant with me was far more self-possessed and gentlemanly. It took a long time to handcuff and bind us. It may have been two hours. Mrs. Page's right hand was fastened to my left hand. Our ankles were fastened, and ropes fastened us to the bed. As I sat beside the attendant, who had charge of me, I stroked his wrist. He remained with us until we were taken into my room. I did not see him afterwards. I heard the conversation between the man who had charge of Mr. Whittelsey and the ladies ; he asked him where his vest was, and if he hadn't got but one suit of clothes; they went to the closet and got a vest; I told him it was no use taking Mr. Whittelsey to the bank, as he could not open it without Mr. Warriner and Mr. Prince. He said he had both of them.

Mrs. Whittelsey identified Scott and Dunlap as the men who were in her house. She knew them by their size, voice, and peculiarity of manner; Scott's nervous manner and peculiarity of shoulders. Have seen him since, at the Town Hall and the jail. Once since his arrest, while behind Scott, I noticed that peculiarity of the shoulders and the shrug which I saw that night. Dunlap's voice is like that of my attendant that night, and his manner is like his, quiet and self-possessed. The next morning spoke of the stroking of my attendant's hand. This evidence (as to the stroking of the hand) was withdrawn by the prosecution, by leave of the court, to which Mr. Bond objected and saved an exception. He said he wished to "save whatever rights we have, but didn't know as we had any."

Mrs. Whittelsey then testified to noticing the grass in the rear of the house, near some bushes, in July or August, 1875, flattened, as if a person had laid upon it. Saw it only one time, and spoke to Mr. Whittelsey about it.

Cross-examined. My attendant wore a light mask; not a white one; think it was one of the masks shown here. There was but little conversation between the men when in the house. The tall man gave directions. As we passed through the hall we saw Mr. Whittelsey sitting on the sofa with one or two attendants. This was about 3 o'clock. The gags were applied between 3 and 4 o'clock. We were not gagged until long after we were bound. The tall man seemed very nervous and impatient, and one time, when we were talking with our guard, said "hush." He had a long linen duster and a white mask fitting very smoothly over his head. They were very cautious about their lanterns. They were placed in position, and ordered to be careful about turning around with their lanterns. Have seen two of these men since, in the chapel at the jail. Think the tall one was the one who came into my room and led me out. The other one I identified by his general manner. The tall one I noticed by the shrug of the shoulders. The one who had charge of us was perfectly self-possessed, and much more gentlemanly than any of the others. The tall man was very impatient and imperative in his tones. In the morning, when we were released, we found the different costumes they had worn, their masks, etc. They first came to the house between 12 and 1 o'clock. They were in the house more than an hour, and Scott and Dunlap were in our presence all the time. I saw the men in the chapel only a few minutes. I afterwards heard them talking in the jail for a considerable time. I then recognized the voices of both. I think of nothing except what I have stated which leads me to identify the prisoners. I don't remember my language at the examination; think I spoke of the shrug of the shoulders then. Am not positive what I said about Dunlap's voice. I only know it was a medium voice, and very pleasant, and with his gentlemanly manner impressed me very much. I don't remember who wore the cambric mask.

Mrs. Page. This witness was formerly Miss Mattie C. White. She was an inmate of Mr. Whittelsey's house at the time of the burglary. She testified as follows: I was awakened between 12 and 1 in the morning, by some one coming into my room, and I screamed. He told me to keep quiet, and requested me to get up. I begged of him to let me remain where I was, but he said no. I then got up and went into the room where Mrs. Whittelsey was, and we were handcuffed together. Some one in the room asked where the young lady went; he immediately replied, "Here she is," looking at me. Shortly after, Mr. Whittelsey, Mrs. Whittelsey and myself were ordered to dress, and after we dressed we were placed in chairs at the other side of the room. I asked him what time it was; he took his watch out of his pocket, and remarked it was shortly after 12. Mrs. Page was positive in identifying Scott and Dunlap. Scott's light, general bearing, and shrug of the shoulders made a strong impression on her mind that night, and she had never forgotten it. He was impulsive and not self-possessed, while Dunlap, when he had charge of herself and Mrs. Whittelsey, was entirely cool and gentlemanly. On seeing them at the jail chapel, she recognized them both by their appearance and their voices, and when the examination took place before the magistrate, these impressions were confirmed.

Charles Shuler, clerk of the Wyoming Valley Hotel, at Wilkesbarre, Pa., exhibited the hotel register for 1875,- and under date of August 5, was recorded the name, " R. C. Hill, Boston." Thought he saw the party sign his name. Do not know Scott or Dunlap. The name of Wm. D. Edson is also recorded in the registry, below Hill's. Paid 40 cents for a telegram sent to or by R. C. Hill.

Edson, recalled. Identified his signature on the hotel register. Also identified the signature of R. C. Hill as the signature of Dunlap.

R. E. Jamison, telegraph operator at Wilkesbarre, exhibited several original telegrams sent from that place, August 5, 1875. Did not know who wrote them, or whether there was any reply.

Edson, recalled. Shown one of the telegrams, and asked whose handwriting it was. Said it was Dunlap's. (Objected to and exceptions taken.) The District Attorney read the telegram :

WILKESBARRE, Pa., Aug. 5, 1875.

To W. L. Edwards, 241 West Fifty-second street, New York.
Come to-morrow. R. C. HILL.

James L. Warriner, Vice President of the Northampton Bank, testified to seeing Edson in the bank in the autumn of 1875. Gave him the keys of the vault to file. That was in the latter part of November, 1875. Think it was the 22d. He took them into the directors' room, and kept them about ten minutes. This was before the new dials were put on. Had a talk with Edson about the combination and who had it. He said it was not safe for the young clerk to have it. Afterward there was a change made in the distribution of the combination, Mr. Whittelsey taking the whole of it. Edson knew of this change.

Afternoon—Wednesday.

West Sexton, clerk of the Rockingham House, Springfield. Scott came there with another man in February, 1876. They came with a pair of horses and wagon ; stopped over night, arising between four and six o'clock and leaving the next morning ; did not give any account of where they came from, or where they were going. They took supper. I identify Scott by his countenance. Saw a Mr. Clark in the hotel about that time.

Scott had a moustache, but no whiskers ; the moustache was not a heavy one. The day after Scott left there was a heavy, thick-set man of medium height asked for him. I did not know him.

Cross-examined. Did not see the men arrive. Saw them after they were in the house. Saw them while there about an hour. That was all the time I saw them. Looked the team over very carefully, perhaps more carefully than the men.

Capt. E. C. Clark. livery-stable keeper at Northampton. Was at the Rockingham House, Springfield, February 9, 1876. Was there only once.

Thomas A. Gallagher, one of Pinkerton's detectives. Have known Scott since November, 1876 ; have watched him for days at a time ; have noticed a peculiar shrug of his shoulders when he walked. It was a habit. He refused to give his name when arrested and brought before a Philadelphia magistrate, February 14, 1877 ; was present when he was arrested, and present when he was before the magistrate. Was on the train when they were arrested. Scott and Dunlap were on their way to Richmond, and were to go by different routes to Washington. There was a small hand-sack in the car when they were arrested, and Scott was asked if it belonged to him, and he nodded his head, as if to say yes. Objection was made to witness stating what was in the bag.

Cashier Whittelsey produced the records of the bank, to prove its legal organization.

L. B. Williams, one of the directors of the Northampton Bank, testified to going to New York in 1876 to see about the stolen funds. Had a meeting with Connors, by arrangement of Edson.

Oscar Edwards, President of the Bank, testified that he had noticed a peculiarity about Scott's shrugging his shoulders. Noticed it in the town hall, during the examination. Sat behind him there, and within a few feet of him.

H. R. Hinckley, a director of the Bank, had also noticed the shrug of Scott's shoulders. Saw it at the town hall.

The Evidence All In.

At this point, the District Attorney announced that the government rested the case. Mr. Bond then said that without proceeding with any evidence. he desired to file the depositions, several of which he handed to the Clerk. He announced that the defense would not offer any evidence, nor make any argument to the jury. The District Attorney, Mr. Gillett, Mr. Delano and the bank officers then held a short consultation, after which Mr. Gillett, in view of the anomalous position in which they had been placed by the refusal of the defense to offer either evidence or argument, while having, as well known, a large crowd of witnesses in attendance, asked the court for a few minutes for consultation. The Judge granted the request, and announced a recess of 15 minutes.

The counsel for the prosecution, accompanied by the bank officers, then retired from the court-room, and returned after an absence of 15 minutes, when Mr. Gillett at once proceeded to address the court and the jury.

Argument of Mr. Gillett.

May it Please your Honor, Mr. Foreman, and Gentlemen of the Jury.

It has never been my misfortune to address a jury of my country, under circumstances quite so embarrassing as at this present moment. We have an important case, begun on Monday, with every probability of its extending through the week. I had supposed that, by the request and courtesy of the learned District Attorney. who has asked me to render such assistance as I could in the case, I should have an opportunity, fitly to the occasion, to prepare some brief, and to present to you some considered thoughts. At all events. I was sure, what the counsel so well understood, it devolving on the government to close the case, that arguments and suggestions bearing upon it would be abundantly presented. as an attempt was made to reply to the arguments of the defendants. But suddenly, unexpectedly, we find that the defendants say they have nothing more to say. This array of witnesses is silent ; eloquent counsel are silent. Perhaps it might behoove the government to be silent, too. I don't think so, especially taking into account the dramatic scene we witnessed here this morning. You will remember that the senior counsel in this case, who came down here among us, from the eminences of the profession in Boston, apparently, and I say apparently and speciously, assumed to desert the case, because, forsooth, he had been unfairly treated in the investigation of affairs.

Gentlemen, you believe that that was mere strategy and pretense. The learned gentleman had followed his client through these mazes, till at last hope went out, and he saw that the ship was sinking, and with prudent caution made some pretense by which he could escape from the wreck. . There is no other construction to be placed upon it. Not a young man, trying a case before a court for the first time and suddenly surprised ; but an old veteran at the bar, trying his case before a learned court, with wisdom and experience, knowing too that the fact of any misruling or any fault of the court here, was to be transferred to the Supreme Court, where everything could be revised, It was not because he did not expect a fair trial. He knew that if it could be of any service, or if he supposed it could be of any service to his clients to remain here, if he supposed their case was not desperate and everything past surgery, it would be ignominious for him to desert it, and he left the court house simply because it was the most wise and the most prudent thing he could do in behalf of his clients.

And when the second act of this farce was attempted to be played off upon us by a second abandonment of the case, it didn't seem to the counsel for the government that it was quite fair to the large interests of the community, that they should leave the case, at least without making some suggestions, in hope that they should be a guide or an assistance in aiding the jury to come to some correct conclusion ; that the defendants should not escape under the dust and smoke which their counsel has excited. And for this reason, gentlemen, I propose, in a very plain way, and in a very brief way, to offer some suggestions why you should find a verdict of guilty against these two defendants, Scott and Dunlap.

I recognize the burden that is assumed by the commonwealth, and that is to prove that the defendants are guilty beyond any reasonable doubt. I assume that they are entitled, as every defendant is entitled, no matter what has been his past history of infamy, and no matter how enormous have been his offences, he is entitled, they are entitled, to every benefit which the law gives to any criminal ; that the assumption is that they are innocent, that they come with that shield over their heads, turning every way to protect them till it is thrust aside by the hand of testimony. But, gentlemen, assuming this burden, assuming all that the law places upon us, we say that the government has a case here that is clear and indisputable. And when it is said that a defendant must be proved to be guilty beyond a reasonable doubt, gentlemen, there is no mystery about that. Sometimes the suggestion is made that jurors, when they leave their homes and come to the court house, and assume the responsibilities of jurors, they are to lay aside, for the time being, some of the attributes and faculties which are to control their judgments and their decisions in the common pursuits of life. Not at all. You are selected to act here in order that you may bring precisely that same wisdom and that same common sense that you do apply to every-day affairs and circumstances. I have heard, perhaps you have heard, sometimes, after some important trial, or some not important trial, a juryman say : " I hadn't any doubt about the defendant's guilt. I thought the defendant was guilty. The evidence convinced me that he was guilty ; but then that 'reasonable doubt !' It wan't proved to my mind beyond a reasonable doubt." Gentlemen, when evidence is sufficient to satisfy your reason and your judgment conclusively, in the same way that it would satisfy your reason and your judgment in regard to any affairs of importance, it is sufficient to satisfy your reason and judgment in a criminal case : and no man, either of wisdom, or sense, or first-rate nonsense, will presume that any different laws of evidence, any different conviction of the mind and the judgment, are required in coming to any decision upon any important subject which shall affect your own property or your own safety.

Now, gentlemen, you come to the consideration of the facts of the case. The evidence seems to divide itself into two parts : first, the evidence of those persons who live in Northampton and in its immediate vicinity ; and second, the evidence of an accomplice in this matter by the name of Edson ; and in considering this we propose in the first place to ask you to give your attention to the consideration of the testimony of Edson. There are a few facts in the case that are undisputed. It appears that on the 25th of January, 1876, the family of Mr. Whittelsey, residing in this quiet town, retired to their beds at night, entitled to the tranquility which sleep brings to the honest labor, toil and fatigue of the day. About midnight, a band of masked ruffians entered the dwelling house by means of false keys. Finding themselves in the interior, they move quietly up the stairs to where the family are sleeping, and suddenly a crash from heavy sledge hammers breaks down the doors, and the occupants are confronted by these masked men. You know the scene that followed. They are handcuffed, they are gagged, they are bound hand and foot, they are threatened. One of the parties, Mr. Whittelsey, who had in his knowledge facts essential to the breaking of the bank, has them extorted from him by brutality, by the wringing of the ears, by the choking of the throat, by the application of torture to the chest, and after remaining in the house for a while, a part of them depart, leaving the house in sentinelship. The next morning the bank is found to have been entered, and ultimately it appears that it has been plundered of a million dollars' worth of property. The question is, who did it? If we need positive evidence on this point, we have it. We have the confession of Scott and Dunlap, made over and over again to a man by the name of Edson; we have the confession of these men made to this man. But I suppose it will be claimed that it is not, has not been, believed, and that you are to put no confidence in him, because he is an accomplice.

Now, gentlemen, the law provides that an accomplice not only may be a witness, but the law provides also that the jury has the right to convict a man of murder, or of any other crime, upon the evidence of an accomplice solely; but I presume, and the books recommend, that the court so advise the jury that it is not safe for them to convict a citizen of crime upon the exclusive evidence of a party who was an accomplice with the others, equal in guilt with them. And we accept that, and we say to you that unless Edson shall have been, and has been, corroborated in various and important particulars, we do not ask you to convict these men solely upon his testimony. But it is no reply to evidence, and certainly it is no reply to truth, to say that it comes from the lips of a thief. The object of a judicial investigation and a judicial trial is the discovery of the truth, and nothing else, come from what source it may. Truth, Mr. Foreman, is not soiled by the medium that it passes through, any more than a ray of sunlight is soiled because it plays upon the hand of a murderer. Money is not counterfeit—I think the learned counsel who took the cars this morning, will not say the $1500 which he received, if he did receive it, is any the less genuine because it comes from the pockets that were lined with the plunder of that bank. (Sensation.) Truth is truth, no matter what source it comes from, and it is not necessary in judicial investigations—and the only way and the chief way in which criminals and villains are detected, is in the fact that some one of them is false; and it is upon the bad passions and falsity of men that courts are obliged to rely. There is nothing so sacred about a judicial tribunal that the evidence that is to control investigations must be brought from the lips of vestal virgins. Why, even Divinity makes the wrath of man to praise Him. (Profound sensation.) Now I pass no eulogy upon Mr. Edson. I have nothing to say in his favor. I do not ask whether you shall heap obloquy or compliments upon him for the part he has taken in this case; but I do claim, Mr. Foreman and gentlemen, that in the narrative that he gave us yesterday and to-day, he told the truth. What are some of the tests of truth? What are some of the tests that we apply when we want to ascertain whether a man is telling the truth or not? One test is perhaps his appearance on the stand. Was there anything in his appearance that indicated that there was anything that he withheld, even though it smooched him with infamy? On the contrary, was not the fact during the whole of his testimony apparent to you, that in all that he said he was answering from his memory, and nothing else? No feeling afterwards, no hesitation about the facts, an immediate response to every question that was given him, and that too, extending over a multiplicity of facts, comprising the whole period since 1872, down to to-day, so that there was a complexity and a multiplicity of facts which made it impossible for him to have fabricated the story. If he had fabricated the story, Mr. Foreman and gentlemen, he would have narrowed that story to the immediate circle of the facts of this case; he would simply have told you that they confessed to him certain facts, and he would have confined himself to a certain line of facts which were immediate and which were few, and which were incapable of a contradiction. On the contrary, he spread out to you the map of his life, and the whole history of his acquaintance with these men.

Now what is his story, according to the evidence? First, what was his story? Second, what are its corroboratious? I don't propose to go back further than this to show that, according to his statement, at some time before the robbery of the bank in Northampton, there was a concerted plan between him and Scott and Dunlap and Connors, that they should be equal actors and equal sharers of plunder in the robbery of any weak bank which any or either of the parties should discover and report to the others. It was also arranged that Connors, whom we have not seen, but of whom we have heard, was to be the negotiator, rather, of the securities and of the plunder that should be obtained. Now we find that in July, 1875, according to Edson, Scott and Dunlap requested him to go to Bloomsburg and Plymouth and Wilkesbarre, in order to investigate the condition of certain banks, which they had pitched upon as suitable candidates for robbery. The week after that Edson says he went to Northampton, to examine some vault doors. He went directly from Northampton to Bloomsburg and Wilkesbarre and Plymouth, made examinations of the banks there, and from thence went to New York. And when at New York, he met Connors and Dunlap and Scott, and he reported to them the condition of the bank at Northampton. They wanted him to go up again and examine the bank and report to them at the Wyoming Valley House, at Wilkesbarre, Penn. ; and he says further, the arrangement was, "that if, for any reason, I could not return to confer with them and to report to them at Wilkesbarre, during that week, I was to telegraph, and I was to telegraph to Dunlap under the name of R. C. Hill." He said that he went to North-ampton, was detained longer than he expected, and that he telegraphed to R. C. Hill, at the Wyoming Valley House, Wilkesbarre, Penn., that he had been detained, and, if important, that he could go on Friday of the next week, and to telegraph to him, if they wanted him on Friday, and that he subscribed his telegram with the name : "William L. Edwards."

What next? August the 5th, he left Northampton and went to New York, and ou arrival at his home he found a telegram from R. C. Hill, dated August 5, asking him to come to Wilkesbarre. He says that on Friday, August 6, he left New York, went to Wilkesbarre, went to the Wyoming Valley House, and there found upon the register of the hotel the name of R. C. Hill, assigned to room number 27. That the next morning he went to that room, and opened the door upon Dunlap, and that during the day Scott met him there, and that there he recited to Scott and Dunlap the fact that the dials of the bank at Northampton were such as to make it a possible field for their enterprise.

August the 7th—and that was Saturday, August the 7th—on Saturday, Scott and Dun-lap and Edson leave Wilkesbarre and go to New York. Then he says that during the next week Scott and Dunlap and Conners visit Northampton, and that their visits were kept up from time to time through that week, beginning with August 9, for some days. They were about ready for operation when, for some reason, a man by the name of Joseph Locke reported to the officers of the bank that the dials were unsafe. Edson goes to Northampton, sees the dials, examines them, goes back and reports to Scott and Dunlap and Conners, and they conclude that, inasmuch as suspicion has been excited by the report of Locke, they will not at that time make the attempt. But they also stated that, while they were here, they noticed this fact, that the watchman of the Northampton bank left his post of duty at 4 o'clock in the morning. And then, after that, I believe, new dials were made, and Scott and Dunlap informed Edson that if he can secure for them the keys to this Northampton bank, they can make an entrance. Accordingly, and you remember the fact, Edson goes to Northampton. What does he do? He examines the lock and the keys, and, he says, that either Mr. Edwards or Mr. Whittelsey, I think Mr. Edwards, asked him to take those keys and reduce their size, so that they would operate more easily. He says he took the keys and went to New York with them,—they have two sets, of course,—he taking, first, one set, went to New York, put them into the hands of Scott. Scott makes duplicates of them, and, having made duplicates of them, brings them to him, and he and Scott, in Edson's room, operate the keys upon similar dials, and are of opinion that they have got the clue to the bank. We find that fact. You are to notice how far any of these facts are corroborated.

I may have confounded the testimony a little, and if I hope I will be corrected, for I have not looked at it since I took it down. It was November 22. I presume your own infirmity of memory, in reference to some of these dates, will excuse me, if I am incorrect in some of them.

But we find, according to Edson, that sometime in November he goes up there and takes the keys from Warriner into a back room,—and there is where I was confounded,—

takes the keys from Warriner into a back room, into the directors' room of the bank, and there, he says, he made impressions of these keys upon wax, which Dunlap furnished him,—Scott or Dunlap,—which was furnished him by one of the defendants. And then these impressions were taken to New York, and new keys made; and these new keys that were made were experimented with by Scott and Dunlap and Edson. Then they went on and commenced their operations. They were ready to break the bank a little earlier than the actual burglary, but were interrupted.

On the Sunday night previous to the robbery, Edson says that he had a conversation with Dunlap and that it was arranged, or about that time, at all events, it was arranged, that they should go up there on the week in which the 26th occurred, and break open the bank. They went, and the bank was broken open. The next day, in the afternoon of the twenty-sixth, Edson was summoned by Herring & Co., to go to Northampton. He went there, and found the condition of things as has been described; stayed there a couple of days, went back to New York, there had an interview with Dunlap and Scott; and the interview occurred in this way: You will find that Mr. Edson says that Saturday night he put into a newspaper, the New York Herald, a notice of this sort: "Idalia, Monday eve;" and he found in the personals of the New York Herald a notice of this sort: "Idalia, Monday evening, eight sharp," which meant: meet me at the corner of Broadway and 54th street. He says he also put a personal himself into the New York Herald, of this sort: "Idalia, F. N.: meet me on the avenue Sunday evening at eight o'clock. If impossible, Monday evening." The Herald newspapers have been presented containing precisely these notices: "Idalia, F. N., Monday evening." "Idalia, F. N., meet me on the avenue Sunday evening at eight o'clock. If impossible, on Monday." The meeting was on Monday. He says at that time he met Connors, and afterwards met Dunlap and Scott; talked with them about the transaction. Asked them how it was that they took Whittelsey's watch. They said it was a mistake. They told him the whole history of the affair; told him they went to Northampton, how they broke in, that they broke in with sledges, that Dunlap and Scott got from Whittelsey the numbers of the combination, went to the bank, robbed it, went home; that Mrs. Whittelsey was the smartest and coolest of the lot, and described variously the incidents of the occasion. And he on his part described to them what he had seen the next day.

After a while we find that Mr. Williams and Mr. Edwards, two of the officers of the bank, go to New York. They go to Herring's, and they have a meeting with Edson. Edson not only has a meeting with them there, but he meets Williams at the Fifth Avenue Hotel, meets him the next morning, and, as the result of that interview, he sees one of the parties and he tells him,—it is Dunlap, I think,—that he thought the parties wished to have the whole affair compromised. This was February 9. Then he says that about February 13 or 15, he saw Scott and Dunlap, and drove with them two hours, and told them that he thought the matter could be compromised, and they said that they wanted him to see an officer of the bank. He telegraphed to Williams and Edwards to meet him, and they came down. In the meantime, however, he sees Connors, has a conversation with Connors, who says to him that Dunlap and Scott have already gone up to Northampton in order to bring back the plunder. Connors tells him that Scott has already gone to Northampton to bring back the plunder. Edson at once became alarmed himself, and he excites the alarm of Connors by telling him that the bank is upon the alert, and that it is not safe for them to bring back the plunder at that time; and we find that, as a result, a communication was put in the New York Herald, "Knox, come home," and that was explained to us. "Knox came home." And we find that in the Herald, as he says it was. They did come home, and after that he has further conversation with them, about the 16th, and then his conversation is with Scott. Scott told him what had been done, and they had come back. Then he talked with them about compromising. Scott takes out his watch, and says, "I won't string you any longer; they are just about laying their hands on the stuff now." From that time afterward we find that there was, on the part of Edson, no advance in the way of negotiations.

Now, I ask you, if, taking this story together, it is not a true story, and if it does not bear upon its face the stamp and impress of truth? Taken by itself alone, does it not bear internal evidence of truth? Would such a story as that have been fabricated? If it had been untrue, would such a story have been attempted to be fabricated, if a false story was to be made? Would there have been so many details? Wouldn't it have been simple? Wouldn't it have been something within his own reach? Why

ited that very first conversation, in reference to this matter, as to the
Jorthampton Bank, and the interview at Wilkesbarre? The important
·e, gentlemen, were Edson, Scott and Dunlap at Wilkesbarre, for any
? 5th, 6th, or 7th of August? Were they there? Edson says they
iat they discussed the question of the Northampton bank robbery there.
ogether? If Edson is a scoundrel and a rascal, if he has had something
iole series of robberies for years, in and out, and we find him consorting
any purpose, the probability is, and the presumption is, that it was for
d for a wicked purpose; and if we find him and Scott and Dunlap there
itment, then we believe that it was for a wrong purpose; and if we find
pointment, under fictitious names, and in suspicious ways and methods,
that their object was an unlawful one.
·? Were they there by appointment? Was Edson there by appoint-
there by appointment with these men? We go to the journal of the
House at Wilkesbarre, and we find upon the journal of that house, the
. Hill." And perhaps you will ask, "R. C.?" The same letters that
had for his initials. We also find upon the book, after the signature of
i Edson's name inscribed. Was he there in consequence of a telegram?
e telegraph operator, we have called the clerk of the hotel, and we find
ifth day of August, 1875, the following telegram was sent: "To W.
West 52d street, New York. Come to-morrow. R. C. Hill." This is
·am. We turn from the original telegram, and we find the name of R.
books. and if we find that both signatures are made by the same hand,
rding to the testimony of Edson, and you can compare this and compare
iat was a telegram sent by Dunlap. We find also that the other men
here was a person there, according to the testimony of the clerk of the
recall the person, to say that he was there, but he does say that some-
ie occasion' he has seen one of the defendants. Is he corroborated in any
rs in reference to this transaction? We find, according to his own story,
n, if he could get the keys to the Northampton bank, they could open
discovered that the watchmen left at 4 o'clock, as he did. What was
find that Edson went to Northampton, and according to Mr. Edwards
·, Mr. Whittelsey I believe, no matter which—Edson went there, took
ink and made impressions of them in wax; and carried these impressions
[r. Warriner says he went into the directors' room with the keys. Edson
keys from Warriner, that he went into the directors' room, and that
ipressions of the keys in wax, and that he took them to New York and
ide. The wax furnished as he said by Scott. He took the keys, made
: to New York, made new keys, tried them, and found that they worked.
y true? Is it confirmed by anybody? Confirmed by Warriner, who
e him the keys, and that he went into the other room. Confirmed
this fact, that when the bank was broken open, it was broken open by
ad the keys from some source. None of them got any keys from Mr.
f them got them from Whittelsey, none of them got any keys from any
they went to Whittelsey, got the combination, and then they were fur-
somewhere, and by somebody, with all that was necessary to break open
, I tell you, Mr. Foreman, and gentlemen, that fact alone, of itself and
anything else, puts an end to this case forever.
ing. How happened they to know, how happened they to take, the risk
break into that bank after confining in his house only the cashier, if not
was the sole depositary, or that he was the depositary, of all the com-
·use you all of you know enough about banks to know that generally
he combinations are distributed between different officers or clerks of the
one person shall be able to surrender the whole. So it had been in this
on says, that when he was up there on one occasion, talking with
gested to him that he had ascertained that one of the clerks of this bank
iations of the vault, and that he ought not to be in possession of so im-
Mr. Warriner admitted the wisdom of this suggestion, and said to him:
ge the combination, and we will put the combination of
ioor,—Mr. Whittelsey having all the other combinations

before that—we will put the combinations of the vault door into the hands of Mr. Whittelsey and take them away from the clerk. Edson says he did that, and Warriner says that that was precisely what he did. Warriner says that when Edson was there, he did tell him that the secret ought not to be in the possession of a young clerk, and should be differently distributed, and in consequence of that, he distributed it, and placed it in the hands of Whittelsey, and afterwards told Edson, at the supper table, that he had done so. And Edson says, that thereupon he went to Scott and Dunlap, and told them that Whittslsey had the secrets of the combination, and that all that was necessary to be done was to go to Whittelsey. And whoever did go, and whoever did break into that bank, somehow and by some means, had become possessed of the knowledge that all that was necessary to be done was to secure the combinations from Whittelsey.

Another and very important corroboration ! Again ! Edson tells us that he ascertained that these parties had gone to Springfield. He also tells us that they were sent for to come home, and he tells us when it was. Were these parties at Springfield ? We go to the Rockingham House and we find that Scott and another man with a pair of horses— and in reference to horses, you will remember that Edson told you that they informed him that they had expended about eight or nine hundred dollars of the money which was stolen here at Northampton in buying a team in order to go to Northampton to bring back the plunder—and we prove by a witness from the Rockingham House that Scott and another party at that time came there for the night and left the next day, and that the next day some other man, with broad shoulders, came there and inquired for these two men. Is Edson confirmed in that ?

Now I say, take these, and simply these, corroborations of Edson, outside of anything that occurred at Northampton, and there is but one conclusion as to the guilt of these defendants. So far, taking Edson's testimony alone, uncorroborated and unconfirmed by anything that happened at Northampton upon the occasion of the robbery.

Now, let us look at another branch of the case and see if the evidence is not as perfect and as conclusive from that point of the case. Were these the persons that broke into that bank from evidence derived from other parties than Edson ? They were here, and they were here for some purpose. They were in this vicinity. In the first place, we find that on that very week, Mr. Holt, the paymaster of the Boston and Albany Railroad, saw Scott and Dunlap in Springfield. On the morning of Monday, he says he went to open his office doors, and there he saw these men coming across the street from toward the Cooley House. He says in a little while after that, about half an hour, he says then they came within ten feet of him. In a little while after that he saw them again, coming out from the depot building. A little while after that he saw them going down a street at right angles with Main street, and there he saw them meet three men, and have conversation with them. So there we have these five men there together ; and there were five men in that house. We find that he meets them that day ; we find that he meets them the next day. He tracks them from one point to another. He watches them. He calls the attention of other parties to them, and he swears that these are the men that he saw in Springfield Monday and Tuesday. And, gentlemen, this testimony of Mr. Holt is no ordinary testimony. Mr. Holt's business is that of paymaster, paymaster of the Boston and Albany road. He is the paymaster of that army of 5000 men that are in the employ of the Boston and Albany Railroad. He is the depositor and the distributor of their money. He is obliged, as you will infer, as a matter of course, to take this money and carry it from point to point over the road to pay it out. Just the candidate for thieves and pickpockets. He has been in that business for eighteen years. His sensibilities have become quick, his eye keen, all his senses alert. He knows how to mark a pickpocket. He knows when a suspicious person comes across his vision, and when he saw these men they attracted his attention, and he shadowed them from one point to another point, in the city of Springfield, for two days. He daguerreotyped their faces and their figures on the retina of his eye, and he tells you it is there now, and he looks upon them, and he says, ``These are the men.'' (Sensation.) This is the Monday and the Tuesday before the robbery. These were the men and in association with just the numerical clan that broke into that house and became participators in that business. Have you any doubt about that ?

Another thing. We called two witnesses from Northampton, both of whom testify that along at different times, previous to the robbery, they had seen one or both of these men in the vicinity of Whittelsey's house. Now, that these men had been prowling around Northampton for weeks, at least, there can be no question. That they had made their rendezvous up here in a secluded school-house, and that they were persons, burglars—at least, they were no tramps. Tramps would never have left an unconsumed chicken there, certainly. (Laughter.) We find that these burglars had been prowling about this town for a long time—for a number of days, at the least. One witness, whose name I don't recall,—however, that is of no account,—one witness testifies that he saw him up at Mr. Whittelsey's house; that he had conversation with him. He remembers that he had conversation with him, and that he asked him where Mr. Whittelsey's house was. To be sure, he knew where Whittelsey's house was before, but he was caught there in rather suspicious circumstances, and he made that as an excuse for his standing there; or it was for another purpose—for the additional information which he got. You will believe that he not only asked him where Whittelsey's house was, but what is more here, because the witness testifies that—and of course it was in response to a question, though I don't think he was asked in regard to it—but the witness testifies that he told him what Mr. Whittelsey's family was, and told him also that there was another family in the house; and you will believe that that was a part of the investigation that he was pursuing at that time, and that was a part of the information that he wished to secure. Another witness met him twice. But you will remember these circumstances. So we find that the men were about here before the 26th, for some purpose.

Now, were these the men that went into that house? We have the testimony of Mr. Whittelsey, we have the testimony of Mrs. Whittelsey, we have the testimony of Mrs. Page, that they were the men. I look upon the identity of these men, as secured by these witnesses, with entire confidence. Mr. Whittelsey says that he identifies these men by their voices,—Scott, certainly. He remembers what they said. He goes over with the conversation. Mrs. Whittelsey identifies them by the voice, also, as well as in other particulars. Mrs. Page recollects the voice. But the questions were asked: "Wern't you very much excited? Wern't you frightened? Wern't you intimidated?" They say that they were more or less excited, and, of course, they were; and it is for just this reason, Mr. Foreman, that they are confident. It is because the faculties were in a state of intellectual excitement, that they were able, at this time, to remember the tones of the voice. It is nothing unusual. Why, it is the way with all our senses—the sort of sense which the trapper and the hunter gets by slow processes, so that the least sound of a voice, the least trail in the grass, is to him an open volume. To a man or a woman, whose mind is intensely excited, the same effects come in upon them as by intuition. It is when we are under great excitement that effects of voice, of sound, of sight, are imprinted upon us, as at no other time. In one of the law books, there is a case where a woman, at night, at midnight, sees a man thrust his head out of a coach, and hears him tell the driver to drive to such a number, and that is all. And a murder is committed there, and out of fifty persons, at Newgate, she was able to identify that voice, simply because her mind was excited, simply because it was intense. So it is in reference to the vision. Why, the books have another case, where two Bow-street officers were in the post-chaise, and they were attacked by two men on horseback, and, after there had been a demand for money, a pistol was fired, and the party, out of seventy-five horses, was able to distinguish the horse upon which that rider rode, simply by the flash of the light from the powder. Frightened! Excited! Did you ever ride after a runaway horse? If you did, you may recollect, I fancy, although it was not, perhaps, a very eligible post for accurate observation, that there were one, two, or three, particular facts which flashed themselves upon your mind, and you saw it forevermore, as if it had burned there through a flash of lightning. It is because the mind is excited that it takes in facts. Gentlemen, by and by, when you shall come in with your verdict, my impression is that, unless the sensibilities of these men have been so deadened and obliterated by crime that there is nothing left, there will be one word, and the intonation of one voice, that they never will forget. So, in reference to your child; in reference to your friends. Can any of you remember the last smile of a dying child? I hope you cannot. But, though it was as evanescent as the vision, if you caught that picture, it hangs upon the walls of your memory as distinct to-day as though it was printed on the sky in sunbeams. The mind is ready to receive impressions. And when these women and that man found themselves surrounded by masked burglars,—women not knowing what was to become of the husband, husband not knowing what was to become of the trust that was reposed in him,— think you that there was any movement, or voice, or language, that did not sink and scintillate in their memories, and is not there now? And they went there in an instant. Impressions don't soak into the mind gradually, but they are imprinted there instantaneously. And that is the reason why, in an intense excitement of mind, Mr. Foreman, you can learn more in five minutes, and commit more to memory in five minutes, under pressure, than you could at other times in as many hours. That is the secret of this confidence on the part of these persons, and I trust in it.

But they are not without confirmation. There are a variety of confirmatory facts, both for them and for Edson. And here, perhaps, I may allude to a little fact, only an incidental fact, and that was that, on one occasion, at one time, Edson says that one of the parties told him that, whilst they were out in Whittelsey's yard, behind some shrubbery, in the dark, that, whilst there, some member of the family was out at the gate, and suddenly the moon burst out of the clouds, and there they were, and they were obliged to lie there, undergoing some disagreeable torture. Well, we find that fact. And Mrs. Whittelsey tells you that, on one occasion, at about that time, in the same month, she went out into the yard, and there she found prints of persons, who had been concealing themselves behind those bushes. You find that those persons in the house are corroborated, as I have said, in various other ways; and I cannot but refer, because it has been suggested to me,—and I know that there are a great many things that yet remain, and a great many more have occurred to me than I supposed there would. You will remember that they found in the house some masks, and they also found some overalls. Now, we find that Hall, of the firm of Hall & Prew, sold the identical drawers from which the mask was made; and, although Hall does not identify these men as being the men that he recalls to have bought the articles, he does remember that he had seen these persons in his store. And you recollect other things: that the defendants must have come from New York, from the paper, from the flask, from the paper bag, and from all and a great variety of facts and statements that have been made, little and large.

And, gentlemen, when you are looking for corroborating circumstances, you are not to look for large facts. Minute facts tend as strongly as facts of more magnitude, to corroborate all main and leading statements. Not in the single corroboration, but in the variety of them, and in the multiplicity of them—coming from all sources. It is not one, alone. To be sure, this matter of the drawers is a small thing, and the matter of the paper-bag is a small thing. The mere fact that Crafts met these men, on one occasion, in that vicinity, of itself is not conclusive. The mere fact that Mantor, if that is his name, met these men, on two other occasions, is not conclusive. The mere fact that these men were at Springfield, on one occasion, is not conclusive. The fact that Holt saw them there, on one, two, or three occasions, is not conclusive, but it is the accumulation of them. You have seen those minute wires, haven't you, that compose the Atlantic cable ? You could snap them like gossamer, but weave them together, and they make the cable that resists the waves of the sea, and the storms of the ocean, and binds continents together that the ocean rolls between. It is the sum of them. As Carlyle says, somewhere : "Only condense the electric fluid into a single peal, and it shakes the firmament ; but spread it out into single tones, and it is a lullaby for children." We ask you to collect and combine, to give force to these facts, and see, if twisted and twilled together, they do not make a coil which flings itself inextricably about these defendants.

Now, gentlemen, I have occupied more time, a great deal, than I intended, and perhaps than you have had patience to listen to, and possibly with very little effect. At the same time, as I said at the outset, I do not feel at liberty, nor does my associate, the learned district attorney, feel at liberty, that I should dismiss this case. without something in the way of comment upon the facts that have been presented before you. The question is, whether these parties shall escape. It is a question between the Commonwealth—not the Northampton bank, not the depositors in the Northampton bank, although these men have strewed ruin in their pathway,—but it is not their case ; it is the case of the people of the Commonwealth, on the one side, and the defendants, on the other. If they are guilty, they certainly ought to be punished. Your safety, and mine, requires it, and I cannot, I think, close more fitly than by appropriating the sentiments of a great man, whose first words I heard some thirty years ago, when he was standing in this court house, near where I stand now, and although it was the first time I had ever listened to that wondrous voice, those words of grand eloquence are as vivid in my memory this hour, as if they had been spoken this morning. I appropriate his just sentiments, in adjuring you that, "When the guilty are not punished, the law has so far failed of its purpose, the safety of the innocent is so far endangered. Every unpunished crime takes away something from every man's security in his property, and in his life, and whenever a jury, from any ill-founded scruples, suffer the guilty to escape, they make themselves answerable for the augmented danger of the innocent."

At the close of Mr. Gillett's argument, it was nearly half-past four o'clock, and the Judge said he would give the case to the jury then, or wait until the next morning, as the jury might feel disposed. The jurors consulted together, and expressed their wish to postpone further proceedings until morning.

Thursday—Fourth Day.

TRIAL OF SCOTT AND DUNLAP ON THE SECOND INDICTMENT FIXED FOR MONDAY.

At the opening of the court, Thursday morning, the time for the trial of Scott and Dunlap for breaking and entering Cashier Whittelsey's house, and stealing his gold watch therefrom, was fixed for Monday, July 16, at 2 P. M. The District Attorney desired to begin the trial on Friday the 13th, but the defendants' counsel wanted time to look up other counsel to take the place of Mr. Sweetser, and asked for the postponement to Monday.

Charge to the Jury.

Judge Bacon next proceeded to charge the jury, occupying about an hour. He stated to the jury that, in order to find a verdict of guilty, they must be satisfied of the guilt of the prisoners beyond a reasonable doubt. "Not beyond a possible or imaginary doubt, for if that were the case, crime would in every instance go unpunished ; but beyond all reasonable doubts, doubts for which there is in your mind a reason or ground. All human evidence contains certain elements of uncertainty. Nothing in this world can be proved to an absolute certainty, and there have been men who have doubted their existence, but a jury would not be likely to say that such doubts are reasonable doubts. If you have in your minds an abiding conviction that the defendants are guilty, and have no doubts with regard to their guilt which in their nature are reasonable, if you have only unreasonable, fanciful and imaginary doubts, you ought to convict. But if you have a reasonable doubt, if your minds are not convinced, do not come up to a conviction that the defendants are guilty with ease and readiness, and you are obstructed by doubts for which you have a reason, then you ought not to convict. You should convict where it becomes morally certain that the defendants are guilty, and you are morally certain in a case where you have no reasonable doubts of the guilt of the parties."

In regard to the evidence of Edson, the Judge told the jury they could convict, if they saw fit, upon his uncorroborated testimony; but it would not be safe to do so, and they ought not to convict upon it, unless it is corroborated in its relation to material matters. "If he is corroborated in important and material respects in matters vital to the issue of the case, by evidence which you believe, then you may believe him." The Judge charged the jury that the evidence relating to Connors, and what he said, except so far as it was said or done in the presence of the defendants, or either of them, must be excluded from their consideration.

The Jury Retire and Bring in a Verdict of Guilty.

The jury retired at about 10 o'clock, and at ten minutes before 12 came in with their verdict. Joshua Crosby, of Williamsburg, who had occupied the foreman's chair during the trial, was chosen foreman. The foreman announced that the jury had agreed upon a verdict of guilty. The court-room was crowded, and a breathless stillness prevailed.

When the jury retired, they balloted at once, and stood seven for conviction, and five for acquittal. After considerable discussion, another ballot was taken, which stood eleven for conviction and one for acquittal ; and after a little more discussion, a verdict of guilty was agreed upon unanimously.

Various Items.

During the trial, the court-room was constantly crowded, every available spot being occupied. Nearly half the audience consisted of ladies, whose interest in the trial was unabated to the end. The audience thus constituted was in marked contrast with the crowds which usually attend our criminal courts. Among the audience were the venerable Rev. Dr. Leonard Bacon, of New Haven, Bishop Huntington, Mr. Gleason, president of the Elmira bank, and several cashiers from Springfield and other places. There were also present, Scott's wife, her sister and a lady friend, from New York ; also, Dunlap's brother.

The prisoners did not seem to be much surprised when Sweetser deserted them. Dunlap's brother, however, who says he raised $1500 by mortgaging his house, to pay Sweetser, and paid him that sum in advance, expressed surprise, and made serious complaint at the desertion, saying he should attempt to recover a portion of the money. The prisoners claim to be well satisfied with the result of the trial. They expected a verdict of guilty, and that the case would go up on exceptions.

The exceptions taken will be argued before the Supreme Court at Greenfield, in September, and the decision returned to the Superior Court next December. If a new trial shall be granted, it will then be held ; if a new trial shall not be granted, the prisoners will be called up for sentence in December. The limit fixed by the law for this offence is not more than twenty years in the state prison.

The local counsel for the defense say it was agreed upon, on the evening of Wednesday, after Edson testified, that no evidence should be put in, and no argument made. They say that they did not know of Sweetser's purpose to retire from the case, until he actually withdrew, and that it was as much a surprise to them as it was to the court and jury. Their conduct at the time was consistent with this representation. The Bond Brothers are pretty straightforward men, and as lawyers are decidedly square-toed ; they are not at all given to trickery or sensational action, and we can readily believe that this version of the affair is correct.

During the trial, many amusing incidents occurred. One day, an elderly gentleman, apparently a stranger, came in with fresh interest, to "see the trial." Taking a chair in front of the prisoners, he sat for awhile, scanning the audience. Running his eyes back and forth and round and round, over the multitude, he failed to detect the distinguished characters who were the special objects of the gathering. Presently he leaned over toward Scott, and asked : "Where are the prisoners?" Scott smiled, and pointing to himself, said, "Here's one of 'em !" Elderly gentleman then spoke of the weather, and it was noticed that he didn't take up the thread of the proceedings so readily as some others present.

The first man to broach the theory that Edson was concerned in the robbery of the bank, was Deputy Sheriff Ansel Wright, of this town. He adopted that theory on the day of the robbery, and before the vault was opened. Within a day or two, young Meekins, the bank clerk, from whom the combination was taken by advice of Edson, advanced the same theory, and without knowing that it had been spoken of by Mr. Wright. Meekins felt a little unfriendly toward Edson, because of that suggestion, and the more readily believed him to be one of the guilty parties. Dr. Fisk also held the same opinion, and expressed it on the night following the robbery and while the work of opening the vault was going on. But the bank officers did not accept that theory until a number of weeks afterward.

wanted. Scott having the right to challenge 11 more, and the government 17, the Judge ordered the Clerk to send out venires for forty more jurymen, to report in the court-room at nine o'clock Tuesday morning. He first directed the Sheriff to summon from the audience at his discretion persons residing within the county, to act as jurors, but that order was revoked, and venires ordered to be sent out.

The jurors challenged by Dunlap were—S. W. Bangs, Samuel Smith, Daniel Converse and Horace Cummings of Amherst, Chas. H. Adams of Ware, Lewis Hannum and Flavel K. Sheldon of Southampton, Willard E. Johnson of Enfield, Harvey Judd of South Hadley, Lemuel C. Graves of Williamsburg, James Porter and Luther Wells of Hatfield, Frederick S. Billings of Goshen, T. C. Davenport of Westhampton, Francis W. Joy of Plainfield, Ansel B. Lyman of Easthampton, Edward Mason and Edward Stebbins of Hadley, Joseph P. Vaughan of Greenwich, Chauncey Witherell of Chesterfield, Geo. Ames of Williamsburg, Lyman W. Baldwin of Easthampton.

Those challenged by Scott were—Chas. M. Combs of Middlefield, Elijah Hanson and John Mack of Williamsburg, Joseph M. Harrington of Prescott, Wm. E. Lyman of Westhampton, John A. Miller of Easthampton, Augustus Moody of Enfield, Washington I. Rice of Chesterfield, Lucius Steele and Wm. Tower of Cummington, E. V. Tanner of Northampton.

Those challenged by the government were, Burnett E. Cleaveland of Northampton, Geo. S. Kendrick of Amherst, Joseph B. Bosworth of Easthampton, Lewis Dodge and Mason Sanford of Belchertown.

Those set aside for having formed or expressed an opinion, or for other cause, were, George D. Eames of Northampton, Chas. E. Lamson of Hadley, Eleazer Howard of South Hadley, Clarence E. Ware of Easthampton, Daniel S. White of Hadley, Geo. Clark of Southampton, Rufus Cowles of Hatfield, Wm. R. Holliday of Northampton, Elisha S. Kinney of Chesterfield, Wm. A. Nash of Williamsburg.

Leavitt Beals and C. Butler Smith of Northampton, summoned as jurors, failed to appear.

The following were sworn as jurors.—Joseph W. Akers of Granby, Nathaniel Dwight of Belchertown, Edward Ellis of Huntington, Francis W. Harwood of Ware, Amos Kellogg of South Hadley, Henry M. Clifford of Amherst, Edwin H. Judd of South Hadley, Byron Loomis of Williamsburg, Almon A. Spooner of Southampton.

Tuesday—Second Day.

The forty jurymen summoned to appear in the court room at nine o'clock, Tuesday morning, were promptly on hand, and after a delay of about 20 minutes, the work of impanneling the jury was resumed. The following ten jurors were challenged by Scott: Harvey Alvord of South Hadley, Wm. D. Boyd and George K. Edwards of Southampton, Dorus B. Bradford and Samuel A. Clark of Williamsburg, Horace Clark and Horace L. Clark of Easthampton, John H. Cook of Westhampton, and Almon E. Cowles and Moses C. Cushman of Amherst. Francis Edwards of Westhampton, Henry A. Clapp of Easthampton, and Horatio Bisbee of Chesterfield, were set aside by the court, for having formed an opinion ; and Nathaniel E. Bangs of Amherst, A. Lawrence Clark of Easthampton, and William F. Ellis of Amherst, were accepted and sworn.

Twelve jurors having been sworn, the jury was now supposed to be full, but the District Attorney claimed the right to further challenge, citing the law which says the challenging shall be done before the trial begins. He claimed that the trial was not begun until the jury was organized, and the presentation of the case to the jury was commenced. The Judge admitted the right claimed, and the defense saved an exception on the point. The District Attorney then challenged Henry M. Clifford of Amherst, and he withdrew. Edwin W. Field, of Hatfield, was next called as a juror, and said he had expressed an opinion. He was set aside. Seth A. Healey, of Chesterfield, was next called, and sworn. The jury was now full, and retired to choose a foreman. As organized, the jury stands as follows :

The Jury.—A. Lawrence Clark of Easthampton, foreman :—Joseph W. Akers, of Granby, Nathaniel Dwight of Belchertown, Edward Ellis of Huntington, Francis W. Harwood of Ware, Amos Kellogg of South Hadley, Edwin H. Judd of South Hadley, Byron Loomis of Williamsburg, Almon A. Spooner of Southampton, Nathaniel E. Bangs of South Hadley, William F. Ellis of Amherst, Seth A. Healey of Chesterfield.

The Indictment.

COMMONWEALTH OF MASSACHUSETTS.

HAMPSHIRE 88.—At the Superior Court begun and holden at Northampton, within and for the County of Hampshire, on the 2d Monday of June, 1877.

The Jurors for said Commonwealth on their oath present, that Robert Scott and James Dunlap, both of the State of New York, on the 26th day of January, 1876, at Northampton, in said county of Hampshire and Commonwealth of Massachusetts aforesaid, with force and arms the dwelling house of one Laura B. Whittelsey there situate, feloniously and burglariously did break and enter, with intent the goods and chattels of one John Whittelsey in the said dwelling-house then and there being found, feloniously and burglariously to steal, take and carry away ; she the said Laura B. Whittelsey, and he the said John Whittelsey, and divers others of his family being then and there lawfully therein ; and that the said Robert Scott and the said James Dunlap then and there, in and upon the said John Whittelsey, who was then and there lawfully in the said dwelling house as aforesaid, and in the peace of said Commonwealth, feloniously and burglariously an assault did make, and him the said John Whittelsey then and there did beat, bruise, wound, and abuse, and one gold watch of the value of $200, of the goods and chattels of the said John Whittelsey then and there in the dwelling-house aforesaid being found, feloniously and burglariously did steal, take and carry away, against the peace of said Commonwealth and contrary to the form of the statute in such case made and provided.

A true bill.   H. C. M. HOWE, Foreman.
S. T. FIELD, District Attorney.

After Engineer Davis had explained his plans of the Whittelsey house and its location, Cashier Whittelsey told his story, and showed the relics of the burglary, being examined more on minor details than while testifying at the previous trial. He mentioned that he was at first dressed in his overcoat and hat ready to be taken down to the bank, which plan was afterward given up, that his pocket-book with some $15 was taken from him, that the front door-key bore the marks of having been turned with nippers, and that Dunlap stood by him with a pistol while Scott forced from him the combination. He could not remember that any other bank officer knew the combinations at that time, but did recollect that they had been changed within a few weeks. He was cross-examined closely as to what was the color of the masks the prisoners wore, and how the other three men who were with them were dressed and what they did. His answers were rather indefinite, though he was pretty sure that Dunlap wore a dark mask, overalls and a blouse, and that Scott had on a linen duster, but he could not say which one it was of those placed on the table before him. Of the other three men he saw or heard little, but noticed them as bringing clothing for the people to dress, and one of them guarded him on the hall sofa for a long time. In describing one of his visits to the jail to hear what the prisoners might say, he testified that he approached the cell by the "back way," using a ladder.

Mrs. Page and Mrs. Whittelsey testified very much as they did at the former trial. They agreed with Mr. Whittelsey that the shortest man of the party wore a black cap with holes cut in the front, making a mask of it, that Dunlap had on dark clothes and a not very light mask, and Scott a long linen duster and a close-fitting mask, thought to be white. The defense made a strong effort to gain further particulars about the clothing worn, but with slight success. The whole discussion was somewhat embarrassed by the appearance among the relics of an extra burglar cap, never before presented in court, of which no one could give any account. Mrs. Whittelsey stated that at one time there were five lanterns burning in her room, so that it was very light, also that the summer before she noticed a small part of the grass back of the quince bushes in the garden was very much beaten down, as though some tramp had slept there.

The testimony of Paymaster Holt excited considerable interest, because the government insisted on knowing what is the average monthly pay-roll of the Boston and Albany Railroad. The defense took exception to the question, the superintendent of the River road sitting by meanwhile awaiting the answer. The Judge ruled the question in, and the reply was, "Over 2500 men for every month in the year."

E. A. Hall, clothing dealer of Springfield, was next called, and, though he could not identify the prisoners as having bought certain articles of the clothing shown, which he said was from his stock, he remembered selling such articles to two strangers just before the robbery, and knew that he had seen Dunlap somewhere before his arrest.

David W. Crafts. This witness testified to seeing a man who resembled Scott, on Elm street, in January, 1876, and afterward saw the same man on Main street, near Maynard & Brooks' store. Witness acknowledged to Mr. Bond that he told him in a conversation awhile ago that he had doubts about its being Scott.

Wednesday—Third Day.

James O. Mantor. Live on Elm street. In winter of 1876, saw two men standing, talking, near Whittelsey's. They passed on as I came along; about 7½ o'clock, in the evening, early in January previous to robbery. One dressed in long overcoat, soft hat, crushed in at top. One taller than the other. Men had no beard, except moustache. Facing Whittelsey's house, making gestures toward the house. My impression is that Scott was the man I saw there. Shouldn't want to swear to it, but that is my impression.

Cross-examined. Cannot describe one of the men at all. The other wore a soft, military hat, and had no beard.

Benjamin Franklin. Superintendent of Pinkerton's detective agency in Philadelphia. Scott and Dunlap were on the train going South. Arrested them in the car, at Philadelphia depot. Had a warrant. They said they were not Scott and Dunlap; that there was a mistake. I insisted on their getting out of the car. Witness was asked as to what he found. Defense objected. Same evidence was offered at previous trial, and ruled out. Judge said that if what they found there could be connected with the offense charged, he should admit it, but he did not think it was enough that the articles found were similar to those found at Whittelsey's. Prosecution claimed that the implements found in the bag in the possession of the prisoners when arrested, were the identical implements used in breaking into the house. Judge admitted the evidence. Defense excepted. The bag was opened by witness, and a pair of nippers found in it ; also two skeleton keys. These were found in the bag at the time of the arrest. The key found on Scott opened the bag. Examined the bag within an hour after the arrest, and before it went out of my possession. Have seen Scott write. Shown a specimen of Scott's handwriting—an order for the money found in his possession. Saw Scott write the order, and Dunlap signed it.

Cross-examined. When arrested, bag was in the end of the forward car. Two other bags were also found with them. The key found on Scott opened the bag containing the nippers and skeleton keys. A key found on Dunlap opened one of the bags, and a key found on Scott opened the other. Bags were opened at my office, a mile and a half to two miles from the depot. Two or three officers with me as assistants. Had a warrant when arrests were made. I made the complaint. Magistrate filled out the warrant. Dunlap said nothing about his name—only Scott. In the bag was a hotel receipt, from the Grand Central ; also another from the Hot Springs. The two bags were sent to the New York office. Evidence as to the contents of the two bags was ruled out.

Ansel Wright, Deputy Sheriff. Found a wrapper at the school-house bearing the printed card of Hall & Prew, of Springfield. Found eight army blankets, a valise containing bits, &c., chicken, bread, rope, pulley blocks, two railway guides ; also a paper bag containing cooked chicken; the bag bore the imprint of the Stamford (Ct.) restaurant, distant about forty miles from New York.

Thomas A. Gallagher. A Pinkerton detective. Was present at the time of the arrest. Arrived in Philadelphia—found Pinkerton and others on the platform. Defendants were ordered off the train. Either Scott or Dunlap said, "You must be mistaken, gentlemen." Saw the small bag or satchel under the seat where Scott sat in the car. Bag taken out of the car by the porter. Asked, addressing Scott, "Does this bag belong to you, Bob ?" and he nodded his head in assent. At the examination, Scott was asked his name, and he refused to give it, saying it was part of his defense. Have seen defendants frequently. Scott had a peculiar habit of shrugging his shoulders, as if his clothes didn't fit him. It was a regular habit.

Cross-examined. My age is 22 or 23. Been in New York three years. Lived in Chicago previously. Sold dry goods. In October, 1872, went to New York; since then in the detective business. Came from Glasgow, Scotland, in 1870. Sent to New York by Detective Pinkerton of Chicago. Known the defendants since Oct. 16, 1876. Know nothing about the bags.

Questioned by the District Attorney. First saw defendants corner of Washington and McDougall streets. Came out of No. 3, North Washington square, a private boarding-place. They were in company with "Wm. Connors, a New York thief."

Henry M. Potter, Deputy Sheriff. Brought the sledges, overalls, masks, rubbers, &c., found at Whittelsey's house, to my office, the morning after the robbery. Among the articles, found a pair of gloves. Of the goods found, a lantern is missing. Found a paper bag, now missing. At the Bridge-street school-house, found articles the day before the robbery. School-house four to five rods from the main road, and considerably distant from houses. Found there blankets, satchel, bits, ropes, pulleys, chicken, bread, and a bottle of whisky. Whisky bottle produced, having label of a New York firm. Found there a copy of the New York Sun, dated December 22, 1875.

Wm. D. Edson's Testimony.

At 10 minutes before 11, *Wm. D. Edson* was called, and there was a rustle in the audience. He testified as follows :—

My age is 52 years. Am a resident of New York. At present am in no business ; formerly was employed by Herring & Co. in the safe business. Have known Scott and Dunlap since September, 1873. First met Dunlap at Wm. Connors', on Houston street, N. Y. Saw Scott and Dunlap at my house. Saw Scott in March, 1874 ; think he came where I was stabling, on a Sunday evening. Saw Scott and Dunlap at my house two or three weeks later. Saw them again, on the Sunday week or the Sunday two weeks, at my house, at my home, in the morning. Saw Dunlap the following Monday or Tuesday, on 4th avenue, near 17th street. Have no recollection of seeing either of them again until fall, when Dunlap came to my house, one Sunday afternoon. Saw him and Scott a day or two later. Saw Scott the following Saturday, at University place. Saw both not long afterward. Didn't see them again until November. Scott then came to see me. From that time, had frequent interviews with them almost every day or two. These interviews continued until the latter part of January, 1875. Saw Scott in February. Saw nothing more of either of them until April. Saw them in April and May, now and then, at intervals of a week or ten days. Had interviews with both on Saturday, July 29, 1875, at my house. Told them I was coming to Northampton on Monday. Spoke at that interview of a trip that I made at their request to Wilkesbarre, and other places. They wished me to meet them at Wilkesbarre, and wanted me to look at the Northampton National Bank. Nothing was said about that bank prior to that time. Told them I would do so, and would meet them at Wilkesbarre. Told them I was going to Northampton, to sell a safe to the First National Bank. Told them in case I could not meet them at Wilkesbarre, I would telegraph them there, in the name of R. C. Hill. I came to Northampton, saw the bank people, and was detained so that it was impossible for me to go to Wilkesbarre. Consequently telegraphed them as arranged, at the Wyoming Valley House. I left Northampton Thursday evening, and on reaching home found a telegram from R. C. Hill. Went to Wilkesbarre, Friday afternoon. Found name of R. C. Hill registered at the hotel. That was on the 6th of August. Witness was shown the hotel register, and identified it. Saw name of R. C. Hill registered on the 5th. Registered my own name. That was August 5, 1875. The name of R. C. Hill was also registered on the 1st of August. I was there the week previous, on Thursday. Saw them at room No. 27. Found Dunlap lying on the bed. Scott was in Pittston. Scott returned, and met them both. Told them I had been to Northampton, and had found that a new vault door had been put in by the Northampton Bank, with new dials. Described to them the dials and their mode of operation ; also pointed out to them a defect in the lock. The lock could be opened without the keys, by putting on a false dial. They were particularly anxious to know how much money there was in the vault. Said I didn't know, but it looked to me as if there was considerable. They wanted me to go to Pittston. Said there was a bank there that looked favorable ; there was a good place to take the Cashier across the river in a boat. Gave Scott a set of keys to a sample lock. He showed me keys he had made from the keys given me by Mr. Warriner. Both Scott and Dunlap practiced on the sample lock I gave him several hours. Had a previous conversation about the Northampton bank in New York, with Scott and Dunlap. Geo. Miles had been to Northampton the summer before, looking up the Northampton bank. First heard about robbing the Northampton bank between my two visits to Wilkesbarre. Scott and Dunlap told me they were coming up here to look it over. They told me a week later they had been here. They described how Whittelsey's house was located. I told them I thought the key to the front door of the bank was a long, flat key. They asked me if I knew how many watchmen there were. I told them the bank had one. Saw them in New York on Sunday evening, the 15th, at Reservoir Park. They told me they were going up the next day, and would take Billy (Connors) with them—would look it all over again, and look at the roads from Northampton to Springfield. I saw them afterward. They said they had been there ; that they were in the alley-way near the Hampshire County Bank, and being suddenly surprised, Connors ran and fell into a mudhole in the rear of the bank. They said it would be necessary to put the watchmen in the lock-up. One of them asked me where the lock-up was. One of them was near the lock-up, at one time, to watch one of the watchmen, who lived near there. They said they had been here several times. The witness here related the incident about Scott and Dunlap lying on the grass under the bushes in the rear of Wittelsey's house, one night in the summer of 1875, when the servant girl came out of the back door and spent a considerable time there visiting with her beau. The musketoes were very thick and Dunlap especially was badly bitten by them. They were in danger of being detected, as the moon suddenly came out while they were lying there.

Saw Scott and Dunlap sometime afterward. Joseph Locke, a discharged workman of Herring & Co. had written a letter about the lock in use on the vault of the Northampton Bank, saying it was worthless, and in consequence of that letter, the lock was changed. I did not think it best to go to Northampton, and gave up going, as the bank was using extra precautions. Scott and Dunlap wanted me to go up. It was arranged that I should write a letter about a horse. I wrote to Warriner about a horse at Florence, and then came up. Saw Edwards and Warriner. Stated to Scott and Dunlap that I had been here. I went to Florence and saw the horse. On returning, saw Scott and Dunlap ; told them what I had found here ; told them I didn't think it was safe to attempt to get into the bank, and the matter was dropped. This was the latter part of August or in September.

Wednesday Afternoon.

R. E. Jamison, telegraph operator at Wilkesbarre, Pa., testified to sending a dispatch dated August 5, 1875, and signed R. C. Hill. Identified the original dispatch.

Oscar Edwards, President of the Northampton Bank. Identified four letters and their contents, as the ones received by the bank. The letters have been shown to Detective Bangs of New York, Mr. Delano, the counsel, and one or two others. Their contents are the same now as when the letters were received.

An Expert In Handwriting.

Joseph E. Payne, for 13 years in the counting-room of A. A. Lowe & Co. of New York, and for the past 10 years a professional expert in Handwritings, having made them a study for 30 years, and testifying in various courts, gave his opinion of the order for money, signed by Dunlap and given to Franklin at Philadelphia, the names on the hotel register, and the telegraph receipt book, and the superscriptions on the four letters. He had examined them for several hours, and gave it as his opinion that the writer of all of them was one and the same person. When asked how confident he was in his opinion, he said he had "no doubt of it." Witness gave the reasons for his opinion at great length, and with tiresome minuteness. The superscriptions on the letters he thought were disguised.

Letters Proposing a Negotiation for the Return of the Plunder.

The contents of the letters were put in, after having been further identified by J. L. Warriner, another of the bank officers. The letters are dated February 28, 1876, and October 13, 26, and 30, 1876, and all relate to a negotiation for the return of the stolen securities. They are not written, but printed with a pen. each letter of a word being distinct and separate from the others. The letters were read and put into the case. They are as follows :—

NEW YORK, Feb. 27, 1876.

To Directors Northampton National Bank :—

Dear Sirs—When you are satisfied with detective skill you can make a proposition to us, the holders, and if you are liberal we may be able to do business with you. If you entertain any such ideas please insert a personal in the New York Herald. Address to XXX, and sign "Rufus," to which due attention will be paid. To satisfy you that we do hold papers, we send you a couple of pieces. [No signature.]

Accompanying this letter were two certificates of stock owned by private depositors, which were among the stolen property. This was testified to by Mr. Warriner.

NEW YORK CITY, Friday, Oct. 13, 1876.

To Managers, &c.:—
Gentlemen—Doubtless you have been considerably annoyed by importunate brokers and others ; so have we, and that this may cease we presume to address a few lines. Unknown parties have sent agents to us at various times, during the last six months, to negotiate for the purchase of the securities taken from your vault, last winter. Some of these agents have pretended to be acting for you and by your authority, but from what little conversation they were permitted to have on the subject, we judge that they were persons trying either to obtain a footing from which they might manipulate both ends, or purchase the securities with their capital by way of speculation.

That you had authorized any parties to treat with us for you, and instructed that party to take such a course as the above-mentioned parties did take, looked to us a little out of order, considering the fact that in our letter to you, last winter, we told you how to reach us ; but at least different persons assured us that you had objections against inserting that particular " personal," and they gave us very plausible reasons for your objections. In view of these facts, we will alter the "word," so that if you are really desirous to open communication with us, you may do so by inserting in the New York Herald, instead of the old one, the following: " Hope ;" after which you make any remarks which you may deem appropriate and intelligible to us, or none at all, if you choose. But we will add that we will pay no attention to any proposition coming from any other source, but if the above " personal " appears, we will send you such instructions as will enable you to communicate by a direct channel. You need refer us to no lawyer nor agent, but allow us to make such arrangements as will suit our convenience, as we have the greatest interest. Respectfully, &c.,

RUFUS.

NEW YORK, Oct. 20, 1876.

Gentlemen : Since you have seen fit to recognize the receipt of our letter, we will now send you our price for the return of the goods. The United States coupon bonds and money taken cannot be returned, but everything else—bonds, letters and papers to the smalles' document, will be returned for $150,000. If these figures suit you, we will make arrangements according to our promise, and you may have the goods as soon as preliminaries can be arranged for the safe conduct of the business. If you agree to this price, insert in the New York Herald personal column the simple word, "Agatha." Respectfully, &c., RUFUS.

NEW YORK, Oct. 30.

Gents : In response to the above, we will say that we do not propose to enter into an argument about the value of the paper ; we know what it is worth to us, and we arranged our price accordingly. Those figures we will not reduce. If you feel disposed to accept at that price, there will be no obstacle to a hasty transaction of the business, but if you do not accept, the negotiations we will have to stop. You will confer a favor by giving a decisive answer. In giving your answer in the Herald, please drop words " Hope " and " Agatha," and use instead the capitals " S S S." RUFUS.

Edson Again.

The examination of Edson was resumed, it having been interrupted by the evidence attending the introduction of the letters, so that the expert might return home as soon as possible.

Scott asked me if I found at Northampton an account of their occupation of the school-house. He said if he had known that their occupation of the school-house was known here, he should have been afraid to come. They went into Whittelsey's house by the front door. Some time previous to the robbery he saw skeleton keys in the possession of Scott. At the interview on Jan. 31st, Scott, Dunlap and Connors were present. Next met Dunlap Feb. 8th, on 5th Avenue, and walked with him up and down the street. I asked him if Scott had got back, (from Northampton,) and he said no. I told him there was a strong probability of their finding the property here. He said he didn't think there was any probability of its being found. We talked about the return of the securities. Dunlap spoke of the operations in Whittelsey's house—said Mrs. Whittelsey was the coolest of the lot. I asked if they had been rough with Whittelsey. He said no—they had only punched him a little with a pencil. Dunlap told about their coming out of the bank with the plunder—they took it away in two packages, one a bag and the other, perhaps, a pillow-case, and went down the street. The next time I met Scott and Dunlap, we rode about in a carriage an hour and a half, talking about the property, of its return, and the probability of its being found. Told them I was coming up to Northampton. They wished me to see Edwards and Williams, and see what they would pay. Met Williams at Springfield. Next met Scott at a lager-beer saloon. He wanted me to get from the bank a list of the market value of the securities, which I did, and read it to him. The amount was much less than than they had estimated it. It was from $280,000 to $300,000. Talked in the saloon an hour. Scott appeared not to notice what I was saying. Finally he took out his watch, looked at it, and said : " I won't string you any longer. They are just about putting their hands on the stuff now." This was the 15th or 16th of February, 1876. He said Whittelsey's watch was buried somewhere near Springfield, with other things. Said it was no use talking any further. If the bank people wanted their property, they knew how to get it.

Thursday—Fourth Day.
EDSON'S TESTIMONY CONTINUED.

Edson said he had omitted to state some things. Immediately preceding my visit to Northampton, on Nov. 22, 1875, Scott and Dunlap wished me to see particularly if Warriner had the combinations of all the locks. I did not know whether he had them or not, but I saw Warriner, and having seen the clerk open the vault, I suggested to him that it was not safe to have the combination in the possession of a person so young, whereupon he changed it and gave it to Whittelsey.

I met Scott on Feb. 11th. He told me about his going to Springfield on the way to Northampton to get the securities; said the sleighing was so poor above New Haven he had to give up his sleigh and get a wagon. I told him I had recalled him by putting a personal in the Herald to this effect: "Knox, come home." He said he had not seen it, but saw an account in the Springfield Union of the 7th, that the bank people were making a vigorous search for the securities, and in consequence of that he returned. I said to him he would know what the personal meant, as he once owned a horse by the name of Knox. In the Herald of Feb. 7, appeared this personal: "Idalia, G, Monday evening, 6 sharp." Met Scott the evening of the 18th, on Lexington avenue, and went to a large garden east of the Grand Central depot. Scott said they had returned with the securities. Said Dunlap fell into Mill river while crossing on the ice, got wet, and took a bad cold; that they went to an unoccupied cabin in the woods, built a fire and dried his clothes. He wished me to get a book containing the market value of securities, and to help him sort the securities, as I might aid them in getting at their value. Scott said they should send back certain pieces. Did not see him again until the following September. Then saw him as I was riding in a street car, and got out and spoke to him. Asked him what they were going to do about this matter. He replied that they were not going to give me "a damn cent;" that I had given the entire party away. I told him he was mistaken. He said he had thought the whole matter over and did not think he was mistaken. I told him we had better have a talk over the matter, and we went to a saloon, sat down, and took something to drink. I asked him who the parties were who knew about my giving the party away. Asked him if he would believe them in preference to me. He said he was not positive; if he was, I "would not be sitting there."

Saw Scott next on Nov. 9th. Went with him to Hamilton ferry; on the way, sent back some theater tickets, which I had purchased, intending to use them that evening; went through unbuilt portions of the outskirts of Brooklyn, to Prospect Park; found Dunlap walking under some trees. I asked them what they proposed to do. They said the other parties would have to be satisfied with what they said. I said I did not propose to talk until it was fully understood what I came there for; that I had never betrayed them to any man, woman or child; and related to them all of my connection with Williams and Edwards. Scott replied that it was "all a damn lie." Scott said, "how much will these people give and let you go?" I said, probably $100,000 to $150,000. Scott said if they would give the latter sum, they could have the property. They said "these people wanted their property, but did not want to pay anything for it, and that was all the trouble there was." I told them they were known to all of Pinkerton's force. They said "Pinkerton could swell my head, but he could not swell theirs."

John Leary keeps a drinking house at Fort Hamilton, where I went on Sunday afternoon; found Connors there; went up stairs, and Scott came up. I told him I had telegraphed to Williams that if he would come to New York, I would put him in communication with the parties. Scott asked me what they were willing to give, and I reiterated all I had said at Prospect Park. I said they were in danger of being arrested. He said if they were, "there was one man who would be brought into it, and that I knew who that man was." He said he carried $1000 with him, and if he was arrested, he should use that money to "ventilate old Herring." I met Williams at the Windsor Hotel, and we took a carriage and drove to Eagan's gambling house, 616 Broadway. This was the week following the interview at Prospect Park.

Witness here gave an account of the commencement of the conspiracy. It was begun in September, 1873, and completed in December, 1874. In September, Dunlap came to my house. I had an interview with him and Scott. They wished to know how to use the air pump for the purpose of opening safes, and proposed to give me an equal distribution of the proceeds of any robberies. I have experimented with the air pump on several safes, in the store of Herring & Co., and before bankers, to show its use, but personally in no other way. The pump is used to exhaust the air in the safe, so that powder can be drawn in through a hole, and the safe blown open by igniting the powder with a fuse. A pound of powder can be run into a safe in this way in six minutes. Met in Connors' room with Scott and Dunlap, and showed them how to use the air pump. They were pleased with it. Leary and another man were called in to see it. The arrangement of 1873, was incorporated in the arrangement of 1874. I was to look at banks, the interior, &c., and report to them. They were to find the banks, watch the watchmen, &c., and Connors was to negotiate the securities, if any were obtained ; that is, he was to negotiate the securities obtained from the Northampton Bank, and which were not available to other parties. Connors was to give each one his portion—certainly he was to give me mine.

Saw Scott and Dunlap again in November. They told me they had been at Northampton, and discovered that the bank watchman went off duty at about 4 o'clock. They thought if they had the keys, the job could be done without shutting up the watchmen, as they had proposed. They said if I could get duplicates of the keys, they could get along without interfering with the watchmen. Scott gave me some wax. I came, called at the bank, and inquired of Warriner how the keys worked. He said they worked a little tight. I took the keys into the directors' room, filed them, and took impressions. That was the day before Thanksgiving. Saw Scott and Dunlap on my return, and gave them the impressions. Scott made a set of keys from the wax impressions, showed them to me, and asked what I thought of them. They practiced on the sample lock with the keys an hour or two. They told me they would come to Northampton that week. They made three or four visits here in December. After that I met them on 8th Avenue, as they suggested it was not safe for them to come to my house. Met them at different points on 8th Avenue. They wanted money. I told them I would try to get them some. They wanted $1000. The man to whom I applied wanted five per cent. of the sum secured here. They agreed to give a certain amount. I asked them why they wanted so much, and they said it was necessary to buy horses. Afterward I learned that they did not buy any horses, They came twice to do the job, and returned without doing it. They wanted more money, and I got them $300 more. They were here about a week previous to the robbery. There was a meeting here that night, which prevented them from making the attempt. They came to reconnoiter three or four times in December. Saw Dunlap the Sunday night before the 26th ; he said they were coming to do the job on Monday night. Met him on Broadway, and talked with him twenty minutes. Had an arrangement with Scott, Dunlap and Connors a week or two previous, that in case they should want to see me after the robbery, they should put a personal in the Herald, as follows : "Idalia, F. N."

On the morning of the 26th, I left New York at 8 o'clock, by direction of Herring & Co., and went to Bristol. On my arrival there, I was telegraphed to go to Northampton, and came on the Canal road. Went to the bank. An hour afterward, a workman sent by Herring & Co., arrived. Told him to go ahead and open the vault, which he did. Warriner and many others were in the bank when the vault was opened.

I returned to New York the next day. Put a personal in the Herald, Saturday evening, as follows : "Idalia, F. N., meet me on the Avenue Monday evening." When the Herald appeared Sunday morning, I found another personal, as follows : "Idalia, F. N., Monday evening, 8 sharp." I went in response to this personal, and found Connors. He took me to Scott. Went to 10th Avenue, 65th street. Walked about some time, and met Dunlap. Scott said : "Well, how did we do that job ?" The reply was, "Pretty well." I asked how he treated Whittelsey's people, and he said they treated them well. The taking of Whittelsey's watch was spoken of ; I said it was a small piece of business, and they said it was a mistake and the watch would be returned. One of the men pointed a big horse pistol at the servant girl, which nearly frightened her to death. They asked how things stood here, and I told them what I had seen and heard. They spoke of a meeting of all the parties concerned in the robbery, which had been held that afternoon. Some of the parties didn't talk reasonable. Some were in favor of giving a portion of the money to a New York detective, Witness was asked to give the name of this detective, and he replied, "Radford," who had been seen at his house. Scott wanted me to see Radford and find out what he would do. Connors spoke of a Boston detective named Chapman, and said he was a good man. Radford is a member of Supt. Walling's city detective force. Chapman was formerly connected with the Boston police force, but is now a private detective in that city. At this interview they gave Edson $1200, mostly new fives on the Northampton Bank.

Under this arrangement, I put Williams in communication with Connors. I had a talk with Connors about his going to Springfield. (Here the defense objected to any evidence relating to Connors, but the court admitted such evidence, on the ground that it was competent as showing a conspiracy between all the parties to rob banks, and that in pursuance of that conspiracy, the Northampton Bank was robbed.) Connors came to Springfield, Feb. 8th. Last saw him on the evening of the 7th, at N. W. corner of 32d street and 6th avenue. Asked him if the men had gone for the securities. He said they went on Saturday, by boat. I said they must be recalled. Went to find Dunlap. Connors said Scott and another man had gone to Springfield. I put this personal in the Herald of the 8th: "Knox, come home." They came home in the middle of the week.

Prior to the robbery, Edson said he saw false keys in the possession of the defendants, in a room in the Knox building, on Fulton street ; also at Scott's house. The ones he saw them have were like the ones shown in court, and found in Scott's bag when arrested. Also, had seen them have skeleton keys, like the ones found on Scott.

After the arrangement of 1874, I gave to Dunlap drawings. (Here a lengthy discussion ensued upon the admission of this evidence. The defense objected to it, because it related to an act which was not charged in the indictment. The court allowed the papers to be put in, to show an intimacy between Edson and the defendants at the time the alleged offense was planned or contemplated, and not that they committed any other offense.) On July 5, 1875, I gave to Dunlap, at Scott's house, two drawings. Witness identified the papers containing the drawings. The contents of the papers were admitted. The drawings were of the vault and safe of the Third National Bank of Syracuse. Witness here stated more fully the agreement made between Scott, Dunlap, Connors, and himself, in September 1874.

The Cross-Examination of Edson,

By Mr. Bond, was begun at ten minutes past 12, Thursday. The lock and dials of the Northampton Bank were changed in October, 1875. I heard the change spoken of at the store and at the bank. Came to Northampton November 22, and was here three days, putting in vault doors for the First National Bank. Called at Northampton Bank each morning. Took the vault lock off. Discovered the combination then. It was 6, 12, 24, 48. Saw the young man open the vault, and suggested to Warriner at the supper table that the combination ought not to be left with so young a person. Afterward heard that it had been changed and given to Whittelsey. Did not learn the combination of the inner locks. Testified in New York, last March, that I had no knowledge of the locks on this safe, or any thing connected with it ; and I had none.

Have lived in New York six years. Went to Minneapolis in the spring of '67 or '8, from New York. Was there about three years ; in the harness business there two years ; never there before ; shop on Washington Avenue ; started the business ; did not do a large business ; first year there did not do anything ; named several persons with whom he associated ; wife did not like the western country, and left in consequence. A woman came there to blackmail me. I was arrested by the chief of police, at her instance, without any warrant. The policeman suddenly left the town. Woman's name was "Sue McCoon." I was in Montreal a year and a half, in no business. Went there from Boston, where I had been in the boot and shoe business with my cousin, under the firm name of W. D. Edson & Co. Was in that business there ten months. My partner got me into trouble, and I had to go to the wall or get out, and I got out. Lost $110,000. Did not know that papers were made to have me arrested under the treaty—never heard of it before.

Thursday Afternoon.   •

Edson's cross-examination continued by Mr. Bond. After asking one or two questions, Mr. Bond said that Edson was prompted to give his answers by a shake of the head from some one sitting by. Detective Pinkerton, who sat near by, made a prompt denial, followed by sharp words from both sides. Mr. Gillett took up the case, and there were more sharp words. The Judge said he had not known or suspected that such a thing was going on—Had you ever been married to any one besides the woman whom you call your wife? "There was a ceremony performed," at Montreal. It was Sue McCoon. Lived with her about a year and a half. I sent her off. The ceremony was performed by a clergyman. Lived with her before I married her about 7 months, in Canada, and sent her off about 8 months after I married her.

The Elmira robbery was then referred to, and Edson said he never spoke a word with Barry, (who was convicted of the attempted robbery and is now in prison.) Never saw him more than 20 minutes altogether, and not at Elmira. Spoke with Northampton Bank officers concerning the robbery on the night of January 26, '76. Also on Tuesday of the week following; also the next day, Wednesday, and again on Saturday; on the next day, Sunday; on Monday, and on Thursday of that week, and on Wednesday of the next week. Again about two weeks after, about the middle of March. Next interview was in November. At most of these times talked with Williams. As much of my testimony as I could write down and tell in 4 or 5 hours has been printed. Last March, I wrote my statement off in Pinkerton's office. It has been taken by a short-hand reporter as I told it. Have talked with Pinkerton frequently about it. Have since enlarged upon it; enlarge upon it every time I tell it.

Mr. Bond—Will that process ever stop?

Edson—Not until my memory gives out. (Laughter.)

The first that was said to me about paying me was in February, '76, when Mr. Edwards offered me from $10,000 to $25,000 if I would tell the names of the men who robbed the bank. Had not told Edwards that I knew their names, but had told Williams at a previous interview, the day before, at Springfield. I never let them know that I knew their names previous to that time. On the day of Connors' hearing, told Williams I knew their names. Talked with Edwards about telling the names and receiving the $10,000, in January, '77. Never since or before. It was never intimated to me, nor did I suspect, that the bank officers considered me an accomplice in the affair. Was in directors' room when vault was opened.

Read article in Springfield Republican about a wish for a bank Cashier who would not give up the combination. Went to the office in Springfield, and expostulated; no high words; was not sent out of the office.

Before the spring of '76, accused Scott and Dunlap of robbing and cheating me. That was not all. I did more than accuse them of it. I do not say they put the personal in the Herald, for I did not see them, but I had an arrangement with them so to do. Scott's residence, the first time I knew of it, was 17th street, one door east of 4th Avenue. This was during 1875. He then moved to 108, 24th street, where he remained until October; but the last time I actually saw him there was in August. First heard that Pinkerton was connected with the robbery in February, '76. Knew it positively in January, '77, when I was in New York. From December, '75, to March, '76, I did not see Scott with a beard, only a light moustache. Last saw him February 18. Here the cross-examination closed, and the prosecution questioned Edson.

In March, '74, Scott and Dunlap handed me what was due me from the Quincy, Ill., robbery, $7,600. I asked them if that was all. They came to my house with Connors, and he said they had wronged me. Wanted me to tell the rest of the party that I had got half the plunder, so that they (Connors, Scott and Dunlap) could get more from the others. I agreed to do what was right. Afterward met Dunlap on 4th Avenue, and he said they would give me what they pleased. I asked him what they would do, provided I withdrew from it altogether. He said they would do as they pleased.

There is no offer now existing between me and Edwards for receiving $10,000 or $25,000. It was made, but not accepted. Here ensued a long series of exceptions and objections on the part of the defense. When Mr. Gillett attempted to show by Edson that the quarrel between him and the defendants over the Quincy bank spoils had all been settled, and that they must have been on good terms before another attempt brought them together again. The defense said they were going to argue that it was revenge that prompted Edson to turn state's evidence. The judge allowed the government to question Edson.

After the Quincy robbery, Dunlap threatened me in terms which no one but myself could understand. He said, suppose Barry was to go back on me, what would become of my wife and children? Connors got part of that money, and Scott and Dunlap the balance. Here Edson left the stand, a witness in calmness and shrewdness of reply, provoking and putting to nought the leading and enticing questions of the keenest lawyer.

Lucius Gleason. I live in Liverpool, N. Y. In '75 was president of the Third National Bank of Syracuse, N. Y. I saw Edson in July, '75, (Objection), about four hours' time. Witness being shown drawings, said they were of the vault and safe of his bank.

West Sexton. Keep a livery stable in Springfield at the Rockingham House. Saw Scott February, '76. He came with another man, and stayed over night. E. C. Clark of Northampton, was there ten days after. Saw Scott about two hours. He "took something" during the evening. He did not wear a beard. Talked with both of them. Next saw Scott at preliminary examination. I picked him out from a crowd of over 20 persons who were on the opposite side of the street from me. A man came the next day and inquired for the two persons who stayed at my house over night.

In cross-examination, the defense failed to shake the witness' statements. Mr. Bond asked Sexton if he had any bets on the trial. I have none. Didn't you put up some money on it at the hotel this noon? No Sir! (General laughter.)

William Sexton. Brother of West Sexton. Keep livery stable at Rockingham House. Was in the barn when Scott and Dunlap came. I recognize Scott. In cross-examination, said he would not swear to identifying Scott, but thought he was the man.

John Rathburn. Employed in Grand Central Hotel, N. Y., last February. Dunlap left his trunk in my charge on the night of February 1st. I delivered it on presentation of an order. Dunlap said he should leave it ten days. Witness identified a paper shown him as the original order for the trunk.

Richard O'Connor. I am a police officer in New York. Only know Scott and Dunlap since they got into this fix. I went to the Grand Central and searched Dunlap's trunk, in which I found wax and burglars' tools. Witness said certain parcels handed him by counsel for government contained wax and implements similar to those he found. I also found two photographs. Photographs proved to be those of Connors and Mrs. Scott; cabinet size and good likenesses.

Friday.

Capt. E. C. Clark was the first witness called. I live in Northampton. Went to Springfield February 9, 1876, and the only time that month. Saw the Sextons. Was taken to the Rockingham House by one Wellington, a liveryman. I spoke with the Sextons.

Mrs. Olive Crafts. I live in Holyoke. Came to Northampton, by the 4 o'clock train, on the afternoon of January 25. Saw Dunlap on the train. He was standing on the platform when I first saw him. He entered the car and sat two seats ahead of me, facing me. At Smith's Ferry he got up, went to the platform, came back, and between that and Northampton he changed his seat twice. Appeared uneasy. Wore a dark, tight-fitting overcoat, and a silk hat. Fix date at January 25, because it was my mother's birthday. In cross-examination it was endeavored to shake the testimony in relation to the kind of coat, but failed to do so. Saw Dunlap on car platform at Holyoke for the first time, and next, last week Thursday.

John Whittelsey. Key was in front door on the night of the robbery. Marks and indentations on key first noticed morning after my house was broken into. Have examined it with magnifying glass. There is also a night-lock which is self-acting, and requires a key from the outside. There is none on the inside. Here Whittelsey pointed out the two marks on opposite sides of the key, made by the nippers of the robbers. Cross-examined. Never saw marks on key before that time. Can't say how long they had been on. Key had been in use since 1865. Never previously examined it, with reference to the marks. It occasionally dropped out upon the floor, and may have been stepped on.

Robert A. Pinkerton. A New York detective for ten years. Have known Dunlap 9 years, and Scott since the time of his arrest. Opened Dunlap's trunk at Grand Central Hotel, and found in it wax, screws, papers and burglars' tools. It was February 15. The hotel proprietor, janitor, and two policemen were with me at the time. Went to the trunk when I heard of Dunlap's arrest, in Philadelphia. Dunlap spoke to me about the trunk; said he sent an order for it, but they would not give it up, and that I was having

ed me to go to hotel and tell janitor to give it up when another order
found photographs in trunk. Took diagrams, first time, day after re-
thampton, March 29. I took a valise from Scott, coming from Phila-
t two other bags, taken from Scott and Dunlap, to Northampton, and
riffs in this town.
Pinkerton said he would like to make a statement, with reference to a
1st him the day before. He denied having prompted Edson by a nod
it the bags in the vault of the bank here, and took them out, myself.
.   Four days after robbery was consulted by bank officers. Began
n a week, myself, alone. Others helped me at times—Gallagher princi-
1 at it during the summer, and in the fall had three men at it half the
ructions ; 12 or 13 worked on it at times. Bangs is General Super-
r York and Philadelphia. Trunk was not given up till I left instruc-
I took the photographs, and then went to Scott's house. After I saw
who the photograph was. My compensation for professional services is
on the result of this trial. If the defense were to make an argument
he government wished to bring out the facts. The Judge said there
ne way or the other, and an argument could not be biased on nothing.
n since 14th of February, 1877. First saw Connors on 12th street, near

s, Northampton Bank director. Went to New York, and had an in-
iors, Nov. 1876, at 616 Broadway, under direction of Edson. It was
the month. Was alone. Had another interview next day, at Windsor
. It was by appointment. We walked up Fifth avenue to Central
ly three-fourths of an hour. Next day he had an interview of an hour
him next Saturday morning at the Windsor, only a few minutes. Saw
s arrest in New York. The interviews were for the negotiation of the
n securities.
Work in livery stable in New York, where Scott's horse was kept.
e 1874. I drive a private coach. Knew Scott's horse. It was generally
Saw Scott nearly every day.
on. I did not own the stable. The horse came there in September,
e in the Fall. It was a road horse. He had another horse before this
name. He bought it of stable owner. It had been a coach horse.
es. Supt. of 4th district of Western Union Tel. Co., at White River
t includes 240 offices in Mass., N. H., Vt., and Ct. Do not know
ne dispatches sent in this district for 1875.
r. Vice Prest. Northampton Bank. This (holding paper) is part of
n from the bank, and afterwards sent back in letter. I handed keys of
Le took them, for a few minutes, into the directors' room, and when he
they worked easier. Combination held by youngest clerk was taken
Edson's advice. Given to Whittelsey. We had just received two
They were new, stiff, and silk lined, with larger die stamp than usual.
ears. Examining writing part of my business. I think these are in
hown letters sent to bank by Dunlap.)
n, telegraph operator at Northampton for seven years. Dispatches for
W. Gates, White River Junction. Do not know what became of them.
sion, now.
Ordered dispatches for 1875 to be destroyed. It is a part of my duty
truction. They have been destroyed.
l Union. Paper, Feb. 6, 1876. The following article, which the de-
on frightened them from coming to Northampton after the hidden se-
itted as evidence. They had reached Springfield, when they saw it and
Telegrams were received from New York detectives, Saturday, stating
e securities recently stolen from the Northampton Bank were buried
town, and that the burglars were coming for them. This news caused
The sheriffs and a dozen specials patrolled the streets Saturday night."
re the substance of the telegram sent to him at the Wyoming Valley
thampton and signed R. C. Hill.
. I am telegraph operator at Wilkesbarre, Pa. I recollect seeing a tele-

gram from Northampton which said that the sender was detained by business, and could not keep an appointment. Do not remember the telegram received just before this one, or just after. Have had occasion to recall this particular telegram several times since, and have once copied it.

Opening of the Defense.

Here the government concluded its testimony, and H. H. Bond, Esq., began the opening for the defense. He spoke as follows:—

May it please your Honor, and you Gentlemen of the Jury:

The case for the government is closed. All the work of a year has culminated in the evidence to which you have so patiently listened for the last three days. All that power, no less than the Commonwealth, can command, all that money, as exhaustless as the resources of the Old Bank, can procure, all that detectives, with facilities which belong to the craft, can furnish, all that villainy, such as is unparalleled in this court, can suggest, you have before you. It is a fitting time to pause for a little, and to recall to our minds the exact nature of the case, our several duties with respect to it, the rules of law applicable to it, the different phases of the evidence already introduced, and the manner in which we propose to meet it.

We all agree in the importance of the case. No one born and bred in New England but that desires to perpetuate the peace, quiet and safety of our New England towns, and the security which is afforded property. To this end the government can say nothing but what we endorse. Yet, after all, it is these defendants, and not public security, that we are trying. To them the question comes home in its supremest importance. Right here, upon these proceedings, their future depends. On the one side are liberty, home, wife, friends—all the rich possibilities of life; on the other are prison walls, a wretched existence, perpetual ostracism from all that makes life desirable. And we, right here, are to place them on the one side or the other.

"Trial by jury" means something then, does it not, in a case like this? Our forefathers thought so. Lord Chatham termed it the bulwark of the English Constitution, and they made it a fundamental feature of our own. Pardon me if I recall the provisions of the United States Constitution, Art. 6, of the Amendments. It will serve as the basis for some things which I wish to say. It reads as follows: "In all criminal prosecutions, the accused shall enjoy the right to a speedy and public trial, *by an impartial jury of the State and district* wherein the crime shall have been committed, and to be informed of the nature and cause of the accusations; to be confronted with the witnesses against him; to have compulsory process for obtaining witnesses in his favor, and to have the assistance of counsel for his defense." Judge Story says of this (Story on the Constitution, § 1780): "The great object of the trial by jury in criminal cases is to guard against a spirit of oppression and tyranny on the part of rulers, and against a spirit of violence and vindictiveness on the part of the people. Indeed, it is often more important to guard against the latter than the former. * * * The appeal for safety can, under such circumstances, scarcely be made by innocence in any other manner than by the severe control of courts of justice, and by the firm and impartial verdict of a jury sworn to do right, and guided solely by legal evidence and the sense of duty. In such a course there is double security against the prejudice of judges who may partake of the wishes and opinions of the government, and against the passions of the multitude who may demand their victim with a clamorous persistency. * * To give it real efficiency, it must be preserved in its dignity and purity."

The whole spirit of the proceeding is summed up in the words, *"an impartial verdict of a jury sworn to do right, and guided solely by legal evidence and a sense of duty;"* and the whole theory of the trial is arranged to that end. The judge, to preside over and conduct the trial, tempering and guiding it in an impartial and impersonal manner; the counsel on the respective sides to see that each is fairly and fully represented; the jury to calmly, deliberately and judicially investigate the charges, forgetting for the moment the surrounding world of passion and prejudice, and know only that there are certain rules of law and evidence of facts to be considered and passed upon.

Let us be frank with each other. The right of these defendants is plain. But the one thing some of us fear in the case is that they will not have the benefit of that right to a ijudice. Do not misunderstand me. · I believe you mean exactly what your oaths, that you will try these men "upon the evidence given you ;" of the most difficult things you will have to do in this trial—one of the igs you will have to do in your lives. The working of a man's mind is ess, and we can hardly ever feel certain as to what subtle influences we our judgments. Our whole lives and actions are tinctured with prejusense we are bundles of prejudice. Prejudice is of that insinuating shed for and unknown, it steals in on our minds and biases our judghink we are most free from it. In this no class of persons is exempt. phers, scientists, men to whom we look as models in this respect, are irely free from it. Even our honored and honorable Supreme Court of have recently given us a sad illustration in their position as political bias of party affiliations made the dividing line in every instance, and nder circumstances that should have banished party from the mind. think, would question their honest determination to decide impartially. ions which occur in our every-day lives, the bias, the mental leanings ition, business, habit, sympathy, or social surroundings. Let different a farmer, an artist, a manufacturerer and an educator, come here to of our valley, what would be most impressed on their minds? The away with him the beauty of the waving grain, the loveliness of our the. picturesqueness of our mountain streams ; the farmer would have f the soil, the productiveness to the acre, the crops best cultivated, the nd what is to take its place, and the like ; the manufacturer would be f the different manufacturing establishments, the adaptability of the ges and disadvantages of the water powers, the relative ability of our compete with other localities, and so on ; the educator would see our table educational center, would admire the plan and workings of our ould become interested in our Clarke Institution, would study Amherst oke and Williston Seminaries, would revolve in his mind the various ies, and go away greatly impressed with our advantages in this respect. d the same facts spread out before them, and all would have gone away iressions, owing to the different bent of their minds. Ask a woman ilf to fashion about any particular person whom she saw at a certain mediately will come up to her mind that horrid bonnet, that lovely ous combination of colors, that unpardonable disregard of fashion, eleir made up the person, but which we in our unsophisticated innocence How ready, too, we are to see innocence in the actions of those we s in the doings of those we hate. Let me take another illustration, il pertinence to this case—for you will bear in mind that the case for is been engineered by detectives. And I cannot do better than to make of an eminent writer on the law of evidence—Taylor. He says (vol. 1, imony of policemen and others employed in the detection of crime, with great care, not because they intentionally pervert the truth, but essional zeal, fed as it is by a habitual intercourse with the vicious, and ntemplation of human nature in its most revolting form, *almost neces*to ascribe actions to the worst motives, and to give a color of guilt to tions, which are, perhaps, in themselves, consistent with perfect rectien are guilty until they are proved to be innocent, is naturally a creed it is a creed which finds no sanction in a court of justice." Again, he nething occurs to raise a suspicion against a particular party. Police iately upon the alert, and with professional zeal ransack every place and e into every circumstance which can tend to show, not his innocence, esuming him to be guilty from the first, they are apt to consider his : reflection on their discrimination or skill, and with something like ieu sportsman, they determine, if possible, to bag their game. Innohus be misinterpreted, innocent words be misunderstood, and as men it they anxiously desire, facts the most harmless may be construed into n of preconceived notions."

ion this feature of the case, because we have been told over and over ld not get a jury to try this case that would not be prejudiced. And it is easy to see the foundation upon which this statement is made. One cannot soon forget the excitement when it was announced that the Old Bank had been robbed. People gathered on the street corners, in the stores and post-offices, eager to gather and discuss the particulars. The bold attack upon the richest and most powerful institution in our valley, was the theme upon every tongue. Since that time the excitement has been constantly fed by all sorts of stories and rumors, many false and absurd ; these defendants have been constantly assumed so be guilty, and large sums of money have been expended and powerful influences exerted to satisfy people that they are so. Seeing and knowing all this, we have felt the force of the remarks that we could do nothing before a Hampshire County jury. If that be so, it is but a farce to be here ; this trial is but a mockery. But I have faith otherwise. It has been with pleasure as well as with pride that I have assured these defendants and strangers that right here in Hampshire County, within the very shadow of the powerful institution that stands back of the prosecution, that right here, they could find a jury who would set aside the inevitable mass of prejudice and the almost irresistible demand which has been pressed into the case, and would deal with them fairly and impartially upon the law and evidence presented, and upon that only. Acting for them, that is all we desire ; speaking for them, that is all they ask. Will you not see to it that they have it ?

There are certain fundamental rules of law applicable to the evidence in the case to which I wish to call your attention. The first of these is, that *the law presumes every man to be innocent until he is proved guilty.* This is a good rule by which to test your feelings in the case. Did you when you took your seats upon the pannel, can you now start with that presumption fairly applied ? It means more than a glittering generality. It requires you to take their case presuming them to be as innocent of this crime as you would your own friend, or his Honor upon the bench, and that presumption stands as a constant shield to protect them through the case. It is as evidence for them, and is stronger than some evidence against them. Take for instance the evidence of Edson— and I shall explain it more fully with reference to his testimony ; if Edson's evidence were placed by itself against this presumption, the presumption would outweigh it. Figuratively speaking, Edson would be kicked from the witness stand—and I trust he would land in the arms of the officers of the law where he belongs.

Following from this presumption of innocence is the second rule to which I wish to call your attention, that the charges alleged by the government *must be proved beyond a reasonable doubt.* Most of you have doubtless heard this question of burden of proof talked about in civil cases, and may have formed your idea of what it means from that. But there is a great difference between the two. In the civil case you come to the conclusion that in the whole the preponderence of the evidence is a certain way,—as Lincoln used to illustrate it, you feel like saying " I'll bet you a sixpence that it is so ; " but in a criminal case burden of proof means something much stronger. Roscoe, in his Criminal Evidence (p. 14) says of the distinction : " The difference between rules as to presumptions in civil and criminal cases seems to arise from this ; that in civil cases it is always necessary for the jury to decide the question at issue between the parties, and whatever be their decision, the rights of the parties will accordingly be effected. However much, therefore, they may be perplexed, they cannot escape from giving a verdict founded upon one view or the other of the conflicting evidence before them. Presumptions, therefore, are made in comparatively weak grounds. But in criminal cases there is always a result open to the jury which is practically looked upon as a mere negative, namely, that which declares the accused to be not guilty of the crime of which he is charged. In cases of doubt it is to this view that the jury is taught to lean."

Wherever there is a doubt then—not a mere impossible, imaginary doubt, but a reasonable doubt, the prisoner is to have the benefit and is to be acquitted. That I may be exact in this, let me use the language of two of the chief justices of our highest court. In Commonwealth vs. Webster, 5 Cush. 295 p. 320, Chief Justice Shaw says : " Reasonable doubt is a term often used, probably pretty well understood, but not easily defined. It is not a mere possible doubt, because everything relating to human affairs and depending upon evidence is open to some possible or imaginary doubt. It is that state of the case, which, after the entire comparison and consideration of all the evidence, leaves the minds of the jurors in that condition that they cannot say they feel an abiding conviction, to a moral certainty of the truth of the charge. The burden of proof is on the prosecutor. All the presumptions of law independent of evidence are in his favor, and

esumed to be innocent until he is proved guilty. If upon such proof
iable doubt remaining, the accused is entitled to the benefit of it by
is not sufficient to show a probability, though a strong one arising from
ances, that the fact charged is more likely to be true than the contrary ;
nust establish the truth of the fact to a reasonable and moral certainty,
invinces and directs the understanding, and satisfies the reason and
who are bound to act conscientiously upon it." And our present
y in *Commonwealth vs. Costley* 118 Mass. 24, says : "Proof beyond a
s not beyond all possible or imaginary doubt, but such proof as pre-
nable hypothesis except that which it tends to support. It is proof to a
s distinguished from absolute certainty. As applied to a judicial trial
vo phrases are synonymous and equivalent ; each has been used by
explain the other ; and each signifies such proof as satisfies the judg-
ice of the jury, as reasonable men, applying their reason to the evidence
the crime charged has been committed by the defendant, and so satis-
ve no other reasonable conclusion possible."
l your attention more particularly to the rule expressed in this last
s *are to be so satisfied as to leave no other reasonable conclusion possible.*
is thrown upon you to examine all the evidence carefully, to study it to
you can make it consistent with any other theory than that of guilt, and
s to acquit the defendants. It places your position and our own in
s. Our duties are the same : to insist upon rigid, exact and legal proof
ie trial, to explain, modify and to make consistent with the defendants'
ich evidence as is before us, relying always upon the presumption of
burden of proof. And if at any point we as counsel fail, you as guar-
idants' rights will supply our lack.
r the government is divided into two general classes : i. e., the testimony
s evidence as to identity.
vidence of Edson that the government must in the main rest. He it is
he whole case, and it is upon his word that the defendants will be con-
Edson avows himself to be an accomplice, and I desire to say a word as
general, and then of Wm. D. Edson in particular :
our courts of justice is clear as to the evidence of accomplices. Again,
for I wish to claim nothing but what we may all stand by,) and make
of the authorities. Phillips, in his work on Evidence, (vol. I, page 111,)
justice would result if it were the practice of juries to convict upon the
idence of accomplices, whose testimony though admitted from necessity,
e received with great jealousy and caution. For upon their own con-
contaminated with guilt ; they admit the participation in the very crime
vor by their evidence to fix upon the prisoner ; they are sometimes en-
upon obtaining a conviction, and always expect to earn a pardon. Accom-
are of a tainted character, giving their testimony under the strongest mo-
ind a jury would not in general be justified in giving to such witnesses credit
s regard to the obligation of an oath. Sometimes they may be tempted
wholly innocent in order to screen themselves or a guilty associate ; and
ir has been their participator in crime, they may be disposed to color
eir statements against him with a view to hide their own infamy, or by
riction to protect themselves from his vengeance and secure the expected
trine, therefore, of a conviction being legal upon the uncorroborated
complice has been greatly modified in practice ; and it has long been
eneral rule of practice, that the testimony of an accomplice should re-
i ; and that unless it be corroborated in some material particular by un-
ce, the presiding judge ought to advise the jury to acquit the prisoner."
, J., (in Commonwealth vs. Bosworth, 22 Pick. 399,) "The source of
i corrupt, that it is always looked upon with suspicion and jealousy, and
to rely upon without confirmation. Hence the court ever consider it
ise the jury to acquit where there is no evidence other than the uncor-
ny of an accomplice." Davis, in his Criminal Justice, (p. 125,) sums
rds : "The credibility of accomplices when made witnesses is always
ius and liable to be impeached ; and their testimony, unless fully corrob-

orated by other evidence, is of very little, and generally of no weight or value in the prosecution."

If this is true of ordinary cases, what should be said of the accomplice Edson ? What does he say for himself ? Take his history as he ·has given it—there is no time, there is no place where you can touch him, but he is bad.

> " His conscience hath a thousand several tongues,
> And every tongue doth tell a several tale,
> And every tale condemns him as a villain."

There is no crime which he has hesitated to commit, there is no infamy but he has willingly sounded the depths—and do you think he would hesitate to lie ? We take this issue squarely : that he is a villain and a liar, and independent of the law which would sustain us, we shall ask you to say that he is unworthy of any belief.

But it will be said, he tells his story so well, it bears the stamp of truth, it is impossible that it should be made up. We have two suggestions to make in answer to that ; *first*, Edson can lie better, probably, than any gentleman on your pannel can take the stand and tell the truth, untruth is a part of his nature, has become a habit of his life. Think of it for a moment, from the first he has been false to his family, false to his wife, false to his creditors, false to his employers, false to those who have received him in places of trust and confidence, false to every one with whom he has been connected. His whole life has been one stupendous lie ; and do not think that he lacks any qualifications necessary for him to carry out his lie here upon the stand. And in the *second* place we have to suggest that it is not so difficult after all. We make no question that Edson knows about the burglary, all the facts, all the persons. He has therefore simply to tell the facts as they actually occurred using the names of the defendants instead of the names of two of the real actors. He has every motive to do this. Suspected himself from the first he found it necessary to tell of some one to save himself. It was the most natural thing for him to plan to gain the reward, save his accomplices at the same time revenge himself on two of his enemies. He had had trouble with these men in the spring of 1875, and he now had an opportunity to clear off old scores, carry through another conspiracy equal to that which he testifies to, again rob the bank in the guise of honesty, and take himself to Europe or somewhere else to finish his career. He is just the man to plan and to execute it, and he has done it well.

The suspicion against Edson, the offers of reward, the trouble previously with these men are already in evidence. We shall also introduce as showing the truth of this hypothesis, the deposition of one John Berry, now confined in the Auburn State's Prison for an attempt upon the Elmira Bank. Berry testifies in detail to the same conspiracy which Edson has detailed, says that it was made with him, (Berry,) and not with the defendants, that they then talked of the Northampton Bank, and that then Edson agreed to swear the guilt of any associate upon some one else in case of discovery. It is significant that at this trial for the first time Edson has mentioned Berry's name, as if in anticipation of the deposition which has been on file and undoubtedly seen by him. And he takes occasion to anticipate and deny it. Berry's testimony has certainly every stamp of truth that accompanies Edson's statements, and the only difference between the two witnesses is that Berry is in State's Prison and Edson ought to be there.

The evidence us to the identity is divided into two classes, i. e., that of the family, and the outside people from this and Hampden County. In considering the matter of the identity as testified to by the family it is well to remember the caution which an eminent writer upon evidence gives that "experience teaches the danger of relying implicitly on the evidence of even the most conscientious witnesses respecting questions of identity." Some of you may recall the trial scene in *Les Miserables*. There was the crowded court room like this, and there as here on the question of identity depended the future of the prisoner at the bar. Jevert, that personification of official astuteness comes forward and says he has known him for many years, and that there is no doubt of the identity ; three former fellow convicts testify, after being cautioned by the Court, to the same effect. The whole audience believe him to be the person, and just in time to save the sentence, the true convict Jean Valjean steps forward and saves him from becoming a victim to a mistaken identity. Take a historical case nearer home. Some years ago a man by the name of Sherman was tried in Middlesex County for an assault upon a girl in Medford on Saturday, and in Newton on the following Monday. A week after a man made his appear-. ance in Newton, and was at once recognized as the culprit. The two girls selected him from among a hundred others, and at the trial nineteen witnesses swore positively to his identity. The presiding judge remarked that he had never seen a stronger case of identity proven, and yet in that case the government became satisfied that they had made a mistake. "It is a mere matter of opinion, especially when seen in the night time," say our Supreme Court in a recent case ; and in an earlier case they add, "mistaken identity is a matter of common experience." You have found it so have you not ? How often have you spoken to a person as one, to find out it was another ; how frequently we hear a voice or step, or see the form of a person that we mistake for another. If you have attended a masked ball ; or if you were present at any of the antiques and horribles recently you have experienced how easy it was to mistake a person disguised, and you will bear in mind that these persons were so disguised. "There is one little word" said my eloquent friend, when speaking to this point a week ago, and addressing one sitting in your place Mr. Foreman, "there is one little word," he said, "which when uttered these defendants would carry in their recollections to their dying day." It is only a week since that word was uttered. It was said in the presence of counsel who felt the terrible responsibility which accompanied it : in the presence of a crowded court room, breathless in its stillness and with every ear strained to catch the slightest intonations of the voice. But I venture to say that not one of these who heard it would dare now to identify the speaker by his voice ; and I venture to say that not one upon your pannel will venture to convict these defendants upon any such identity.

But there are other witnesses they say who saw the defendants, as they think, at various times here and in Springfield. We adopt that testimony as our own and if it is true it is decisive of this case. You will recall that the defendant Scott according to the witnesses was here at those times walking about freely, and that he had no beard. If there are any two facts which can be proved in this case, they are that at these times mentioned Scott had a full beard and was lame. We shall introduce a number of witnesses to this point, and shall we think satisfy you upon it.

There are two other incidental features of the government's evidence to which perhaps I ought to refer, that is, the evidence of the detectives as to the plan, and burglars' tools, and to the expert testimony upon the handwriting.

I have already referred to detective evidence, and to the fact that this is a detective case. If I were talking to a Northampton jury I need only refer to what is known as the incendiary trial. In that case it was said by one of the legal gentlemen who has until recently sat with the Attorneys for the prosecution, "they have found rich pastures in Northampton." To continue in this suggestive strain, they are again turned loose into the rich fields of our valley. They are paid to convict, and they are going to convict if they can. And the tendency of a detective's work is most always to throw mud. They must get something bad about these men—as they think they must about the witnesses—and so they put burglars' tools into Scott's satchel, and a plan into Dunlap's trunk. We deny it all.

You enjoyed, I have no doubt, as we enjoyed yesterday the testimony of Mr. Payne. He is a positive man. He has been a witness before he tells us. One of his earliest cases was the Howland will case. Thirty-two experts testified in that case. Mr. Payne was just as positive there. "I have not the slightest doubt, he said," that the signature was traced. Eminent men, among them such names as Joseph Willard, an expert of long standing, Lowell the eminent engraver ? Agassis, who brought to the case his acute analytical skill, with others, and they pronounced the signature as showing no signs of tracing. This matter of handwriting isn't a thing to be settled without doubt, even by Mr. Payne. So uncertain is such testimony that many Courts including the Supreme Court of the United State's have refused to receive such testimony and although it is received in our own State for what it is worth, yet in the leading case (Moody vs. Rowell, 17 Pick. 497.) Chief Justice Shaw says : "It is agreed on all hands that such evidence is generally deserving of very little consideration." It is really a matter for your own good common sense. We shall give you such aid as we can, and shall confidently ask you to say that the opinion given isn't true and that the writing is not that of the defendants.

There is one other matter of defense of which you will probably expect me to speak. You have heard it intimated doubtless of the efforts which would be made to show an alibi. Ever since Dickens' wrote, this it has been a favorite subject of advice and comment. An honest alibi is not always an easy thing to show. It would be very likely to puzzle any member of your pannel to prove where he was on a particular day a year ago.

It is not an easy thing to do. Of course it would be easy for us with detective assistance perhaps to produce the testimony of scores of witnesses that these defendants were at a ball, or at some public place. But we propose to bring forward no such testimony. We have evidence as to the whereabouts of the defendants at the material times testified to, but it is the natural and ordinary testimony which would be expected in an honest alibi. The testimony of the family, of those who happened to be there at particular times, and it is our good fortune to have the testimony of one witness who happened to be there on business the very day this robbery occurred. And it is decisive.

As I have said before it is your duty to reconcile the evidences with the theory of innocence if you can. And you will find I think when you come to see it all together, that the only way you can reconcile it is in this way. The man who was up here under those suspicious circumstances which point him out as one of the robbers, (whom Edson says was one,) cannot have been Scott, for Scott had a full beard and was lame while this man had a smooth face and no trouble with his walk ; that these men so seen about here so much resembled the defendants, would easily account for the mistake of the Whittelsey family under the circumstances of that night ; Edson's position, his nature, his hope of reward and desire for revenge easily reconcile his statements with the hypothesis of innocence. We ask you to take the evidence as it comes in, then, weigh it fairly in connection with the evidence for the prosecution, remembering the presumption of innocence which is a constant shield to the defendants and the burden of proof by which it must be overcome, and above all things we ask you to bring to the consideration a fair and impartial judgment.

Friday Afternoon.

The entire afternoon was spent in reading depositions, and discussing the objections raised on either side. A great portion of the time was spent* in discussing. The court room was crowded as it had never been before, much the larger part of the audience being ladies. There did not seem to be room for one more person. The weather was oppressively warm, and much discomfort was endured, but all braved it through to the end.

The first deposition offered was that of John Berry, alias Meyers, now in the State prison at Auburn, N. Y., serving out a sentence for attempting to rob the Second National Bank of Elmira, N. Y., in 1873. After reading one or two questions and answers, showing that Berry was giving evidence as to Edson's connection with that attempted robbery, the government objected to its introduction, and the objection was sustained, on the ground that the proving of a conspiracy between Edson and Berry to rob banks, could not *disprove* the charge of a conspiracy between Edson and Scott and Dunlap. It appeared from so much of the deposition as was read, that Berry refused to give his full or real name, and that he alleges that himself, Edson and three others were engaged in that robbery. It also appeared, from remarks of defendants' counsel, that they expected to prove by this deposition a conspiracy between Edson, Berry and parties *other* than Scott and Dunlap, in pursuance of which the attempt on the Elmira bank was made. In other words, to show that Edson's testimony that Scott and Dunlap were engaged in that conspiracy was false.

The second deposition was that of J. Jameson Raphael of New York, bookkeeper for, and manager of the estate of Joseph Potter, deceased. The estate had houses to rent, and rented one—No. 250 West 43d street—to a family by the name of Scott, from Sept. 15, 1875, to Feb. 10 or 12, 1876, when they moved out unexpectedly, although the rent was paid in advance to April. He did not know the man Scott, and never saw him, but had been informed that he was the party under arrest for a bank burglary.

The next deposition was that of Silas D. Herring, of the firm of Herring & Co., safe manufacturers, of New York. The firm made two air pumps for opening safes, from a patent taken in the name of John D. Tarrell, one of the firm, to prevent its use by other parties. The pumps were kept in the basement of Herring & Co.'s store. Edson had been employed by the firm as traveling salesman from 1872 to 1874, at a salary of $2,000 a year, and from 1874 to December, 1876, at a salary of $2,400. He was discharged because it did not pay the firm to keep him. A telegram was sent to Edson at Bristol, Ct., on the morning after the robbery, to go to Northampton, see the bank people, and get a certificate from them attesting to the value of the lock. It was then believed by Herring & Co., as it was by the bank officers, that the vault had not been opened, and they wanted a certificate as to the capacity of their lock to resist burglars. Edson was directed to go

to Bristol on Jan. 25, but he did not go until the 26th. On the 24th, he was charged
with $50 on the books.

The next deposition was that of Prof. Jules E. Pstrokonsky, a Russian music teacher,
52 years old. He deposed that he knew Mr. and Mrs. Scott. Gave Mrs. Scott lessons in
music in January and February, 1876 ; gave her two lessons a,week, on Mondays and
Thursdays, at 12 M. Took dinner with them every time he gave a lesson in those
months. Scott was there at dinner every day I was there. He had a full beard all the
time ; "am convinced and almost certain I did not see him during that time without a
full beard." Saw a young man there in January, 1876, apparently a boarder. Did not
know who he was. Saw Scott there just before they moved away. Commenced giving
lessons to Mrs. Scott June 5, 1875. Became acquainted with her at Hall's music store.
Continued to give her lessons until May, 1876. After moving, she resided at 207 West
50th street. First knew Scott in December, 1875. Never knew Scott's business. Visited
Mrs. Scott regularly on Mondays and Thursdays, from June, 1875, to May, 1876, except
one or two days, while they were moving. Scott was also present, to the best of my recollection, when I dined there. It was an invariable rule for me to dine with the Scotts on
lesson days. Mrs. Scott spoke to me about going to Northampton as a witness, but afterward said it would not be necessary, as my deposition could be taken. My wife keeps a
cigar stand. Scott has always worn a full beard while I have known him. Deponent
slept for a while at a barber shop.

The next deposition was that of Mrs. Eliza Ballou, 65 years of age, a resident of Newark, N. J. In the winter of 1876, she lived on West 50th street, New York. Knew
Scott. First saw him in March, 1876. He boarded with us three months. It was "in
March or thereabouts" that I first saw him. Here the government objected to the evidence as immaterial, the time mentioned being indefinite and remote from the time of
the robbery. The defense said that the date fixed by the deposition was wrong, and they
expected to correct it by a witness present. The Judge ruled that a deposition could not
be changed by evidence, and then used as evidence ; it must be admitted as taken and
sworn to, or not at all.

At this point there was considerable talk on the part of the counsel. The defense com-
plained that the court shut out much of the evidence which they regarded as material.
The Judge said, "The government wouldn't get anything in, if I sustained all of your
objections."

One of the jurors wanted to go home on Saturday—said it would be $25 loss to him
not to go. The Judge said he could not postpone the trial for that reason—he didn't
know but he would give more than that sum to be gone himself. When he got hold of a
tough job, he wanted to finish it as soon as possible. He declined to postpone the trial
for a day, and decided to go on with it on Saturday.

Saturday—Sixth Day.

The reading of the deposition of Mrs. Ballou was resumed. She deposed that Scott
had a full beard while at her house in March, or at about that time—am positive of it.
He devoted his time to study while with us. Learned nothing as to what his business
was. My daughter is carrying on a millinery business at Newark, in my name. Mrs.
Scott has no interest in the business. There were several other boarders when Scott
boarded with us.

Patrick McHugh. This witness was a young man, who said he tended a dog and bird
bazar at No. 3 Green street, New York. Was there in the fall of '75 and winter of '76.
Saw Scott there two or three days before the Christmas of 1875. He came to buy a dog,
but made no purchase then. Came again December 31, when I saw and talked with him.
Saw him at his house the same evening. Went there to take a dog he had purchased.
He lived at 250 West 40th street, in a two-story house, with large pillars in front. I entered the house and saw Scott there. Saw him a day or two over three weeks afterward,
at the store, when he brought the dog back. Did not see him after that. In ten or
twelve days, Mr. and Mrs. Scott came for the dog. Know this by the charge made for
the dog's board. This was in February. Scott had a beard when I saw him at that time
(December, January and February), about as he has now (full, but stout).

Cross-examined by Mr. Gillett. Know a man by the name of More. First saw him
here. Do not know Butcher McCarty. Work for Mr. Dovey. Had not seen Scott before
the Christmas of 1875. Sold another dog that day, to go to Pittsburg. I took the dog

to the house the same evening the sale was made. Have been in the bird and dog business six years. Am confident that what I have stated is fact. Mrs. Scott came to see me about this evidence.

In answer to questions by Mr. Bond, witness said he carried, at the time he took the dog to Scott's, a bird and cage to another party, on 40th street, and that enables me to fix this date. Think Scott lived on 43d street. Am not positive to which street I took the dog, nor to which street I took the bird and cage—may have got them mixed, but took the dog to Scott's.

Miss Amelia Wood. This witness is a good-looking little lady, of about 25 years, sister of Mrs. Scott. She resides at Ellenville, N. Y., and lived with Mrs. Scott in New York in the fall of 1875 and the winter of 1876. Went there in July, 1875. She lived at 108 E. 24th street. I lived there with her until September, then moved to 250 W. 43d street, and lived there one month, until January 31st. When I left, they were there. The family consisted of Mr. and Mrs. Scott, Dunlap, myself, and a servant, until after Christmas. Dunlap was in poor health. I thought he had the consumption. Sometimes he took his meals with the family, and sometimes they were sent to his room. In January, 1876, Scott was not away from the house. He sprained his ankle a few days after New Year's, and was not able to be away. He was at home January 25 and 26. Dunlap was there, and had his meals. Scott had a beard then—am positive of it. He could not go out, if he had wanted to, on account of his sprained ankle. I remember that a boy brought a dog to the house—a New Year's present from Mrs. Scott.

Cross-examined. Went to Scott's in July, 1875, and lived there until January 31, 1876. Left Grand Rapids, Mich., where I lived, July 12, and think I must have arrived at Scott's about the middle of July. Scott was not out of the house in January, 1876, except for a short walk. He sprained his ankle two or three days after New Year's, and did not go out, except to walk around the corner; was not gone over an hour. Dunlap was sick. He was there when I went there. I did not see him much at first—was not acquainted with him. Knew he was not well. In October he was taking cod liver oil. Had no talk with him about his health. Do not know that Scott and Dunlap had a physician, or consulted one. I was employed at upholstering by Kurtz & Bro., Broadway. I am older than Mrs. Scott.

The next witness was *Prof. William J. Nævius,* of New York, teacher of the academic branches, history, arithmetic, geometry, and rhetoric, a man of 50 or 55 years, having a marked individuality. He announced at the outset that his name Nævius was pronounced the same as the Nævius spoken of in the Second Epistle of Horace. Mr. Gillett said to the witness that he made a mistake in pronouncing the word Epistle ; it was not *Epistel.* The Professor was somewhat disconcerted at this recognition of his literary acquirements. Witness now resides in Brooklyn, but for twenty-five years lived in New York, and on one street 13 years. I met Scott on the 22d of March, 1876. He took lessons of me, and to my best recollection, had just such a beard then as he has now. Saw Scott about five times a week from that time until the middle of June. In the last of May, I noticed that he had shaved. He manifested serious indications of lameness. When he came to take lessons of me he would take off his shoe and rest his lame foot on a chair.

Cross-examined. After he had shaved, I think he wore a moustache. I was called upon as to my being a witness, by Mrs. Scott, about three weeks ago.

Miss Rose Ballou, of Newark, N. J., daughter of the Mrs. Ballou who gave her deposition. In the winter of 1876 I resided on 50th street, N. Y., with my mother. First saw Scott February 12, 1876, when he called at my mother's to procure board. Saw him three times that day. I went to his house, 250 W. 43d street. There saw Mr. Potter, the owner of the house. Scott came to our house to board ; saw him afterward every day. He had a full beard, heavier than the one he wears now, and noticed his lameness, and that he had shaved during the last of May or first of June. Remarked upon it at the time.

Cross-examined. My age is 27 years. I took charge of the house. I first saw Scott February 1, 1876, when my mother and myself were present. Then I went to his house. Had friends living in that street at that time. We had 4 or 5 boarders. Mr. Schoff boarded there; also, Mrs. Willis and her daughter. Talked with Mr. More about this case. I boarded at his mother-in-law's house one year, until last April. Am in the millinery business now. Paid $10 a week for board of my mother and myself, from money raised by mortgaging my property. Mother paid the rent. Some of the bills are unpaid—butchers', grocers', and rent bills. Quit keeping house in March, and took a room in 18th street, near 2d avenue, for three weeks—near house of Sec. Fish. Went from there to 12th street, and lived there two weeks, and then went to 119 W. 23d street. Do not know Connors. Went to Newark in April last. Raised some money on property in Sterling, Ill., given me by my sister. Seen More several times in Newark. At one time I took charge of a gentleman's house for the board of my mother and myself, for two weeks. Had some money left from keeping boarders.

Marcus A. Decker, of 136 E. 113th street, N. Y., am a piano-tuner for 12 years. In the fall of 1875, was connected with Decker & Bro., piano dealers, the firm consisting of my father and uncle. On December 14, 1875, we sold Mrs. Scott a piano on installments. I was at Scott's house in January, 1876, collecting the dues on the piano ; was there on the 15th and on the 25th, as shown by receipts which I gave, and which are now in the possession of Mrs. Scott. On the 25th, found in the house Mr. and Mrs. Scott, and Dunlap. Was there at nine o'clock that evening. Was at the house the next night. Saw Scott and Dunlap there then. I was playing on the piano and broke a string, which Mrs. Scott seemed to feel very badly about, as she was to take a lesson on Thursday. I was there the next night, and saw Scott and Dunlap there. Called there on my way up from Bleeker street, and stopped for dinner. Arrived there between 6 and 7, and repaired the string. Scott and Dunlap were there. Scott had a beard on the 25th and 26th, a little longer than his beard is now. Have never seen him without a beard. Have known him four years. Seen him in Winters. Saw him January 15, in the morning. He had a beard then. He was lame on the 26th ; knew it, because when I repaired the piano-string he was in my way. Of this I am positive. Took dinner with him on the 26th.

Cross-examined. The firm of Decker & Bro., has been out of existence a year. I am working now for my uncle ; do inside tuning. There was a lawsuit between Decker & Bro. and Decker Bros. as to which should use the name. Saw Scott once or twice a week about four years ago, at my house. Never saw Connors. Did not see Scott during the summer. Next saw him in 1876, when he came to my store on Bleeker street. That was January 14, 1876. Rented Mrs. Scott a piano, which she has now. Do not know that it is paid for. The piano sold him in 1873 has been paid for. I frequently run into Scott's to dine and lunch. In 1873 I learned that Scott and his wife were married. Saw Mrs. S. at my store just after May ; also saw her a couple of months afterward ; did not see her frequently previous to her marriage. Lunched at Scott's November half a dozen times, after the others were through. Scott was lame on January 14. Mrs. Scott was a favorite in my mother's family, and used to call there frequently.

At this point, half past 12, the matter of adjournment was brought up. Mr. Gillett stated that he had an engagement on Monday in a case that had already been postponed once. Mr. Leonard said he was willing to assent to the wishes of Mr. Gillett, and the Judge ordered an adjournment of the court to Tuesday, July 24 at 10 o'clock.

Tuesday—Seventh Day.

An hour before the assembling of the court, this morning, the crowd began to gather in front of the court-house, and for an hour blocked up the walk for a distance of several rods. When the court opened, at ten o'clock, the court-room was crowded to its greatest capacity, about one-half the audience consisting of ladies, of whom a considerable portion were young girls. Mrs. Scott and Miss Ballou, witnesses for the defense, were seated near the witness stand.

Mr. Bond called upon the witness Decker to identify the contract made between Decker and Mrs. Scott in December, 1875, for the piano, and also the receipts given for the payments made, including those given on Jan. 15th and 25th, and them offered them in evidence. Mr. Gillett objected to the admission of the receipts, and the court ruled them out.

Silas S. Packard. I have charge of a business college in New York, formerly Bryant & Stratton's. Have had charge of it for 18 years, and had more or less to do with handwritings for 30 years, Have published works on penmanship. Mr. Packard gave it as his opinion that the order written by Scott to Detective Franklin when he was arrested, and the directions on the letters written to the bank respecting negotiations for the return of the securities, were not written by the same person, as Payne the expert had testified to, and gave his reasons for that opinion at considerable length. Witness also thought the telegram sent from Wilkesbarre and signed by R. C. Hill, was not written by Dunlap, judging by his signature to the order. On cross-examination, witness said the superscriptions on the letters were in a disguised hand, but the body of the order (written by Scott) and the signature of Dunlap to the order (written by Dunlap) were disguised. Mr. Gillett pointed out certain letters in the different writings, and the witness admitted that there was in them a similarity ; in some it was marked. I have been twice a witness in cases involving handwritings, but testified only once.

Julius Davis, of 311 Broome street, New York, a Jew, was sworn with his hat on. Been in this country 13 or 14 years. Have known Scott 3 or 4 years. Have done work for him. In January, 1876, altered a dress coat to a swallow tail. Mrs. Scott came down for me, and I went up to the house. Carried the coat back on Feb. 7th. Did some work for another man at Scott's. Took both garments back on Feb. 7th, my birthday. Mr. Scott gave me a cane at that time. Mrs. Scott came for me on a Sunday, and I went on the next Monday. Scott had a beard at that time—beard was a little bigger than it is now.

Cross-examined. Have done work for Scott 3 or 4 years, and done business for him. Made no clothing for him, only repairing. Been to his house on 43d street several times, more than five times. It was in February that I carried the clothes back. The first time I went to his house he lived in Brooklyn. Cannot tell the street. Do not know the street. Went there only once while he lived in Brooklyn. The next time I went, he lived in New York, at East 17th street. Went there four or five times. The next time I went, he lived on 43d street. Scott never gave a present before. Mrs. Scott's mother and my wife are sisters. I have been intimate with Scott's family, and know Mrs. Scott since she was a girl. Saw Scott on Feb. 7th, on the second floor. When I took them from him he was up stairs. Do not employ any hands. My room is in the basement. Do not remember what day it was when I took the clothes back. It was half past seven in the evening. Saw Mrs. Scott then.

In reply to Mr. Bond, witness said he could not tell whether Dunlap was the man he saw there or not, but he thought he was. Questioned by Mr. Gillett : It was dark when I took the clothes from the house, and I could not see who the man was.

Deputy Sheriffs Potter and Munyan testified that they had never noticed any shrug of Scott's shoulders since they had been guarding the prisoners at the jail. Munyan has been on guard there every day since soon after they were brought to the jail, and Potter has been there more or less.

Close of the Defense.

At this point, 11.15 this A. M., the defense closed very unexpectedly. The multitude had expected that Mrs. Scott would be put upon the stand, and great was their disappointment.

Decker, recalled. Went to 43d street half a dozen times in January, to buy pianos of Schaffer. Sold 50 to 75 pianos a year. Name of my firm Decker & Brother. That firm continued 8 or 10 years. The old firm was Decker Brothers. The name of the firm was put on the front of the piano. Did not manufacture the pianos. Had a right to put it there. Witness referred to a book, which Mr. Gillett had, containing a letter written by witness. Letter was written for him to sign, and he signed it. Witness was asked what right he had to put the name of Decker Brothers on the pianos sold by Decker & Bro. I said in the letter I had no right to put the name of Decker Bros. on the pianos I sold. I was not arrested for that ; never was arrested for any offense or any charge. I never manufactured pianos. A part of the answer I put into that suit was true, and a part untrue. Have been in attendance here two weeks. Mrs. Scott was here last week also, and Mr. Moore. Miss Ballou here, too, and "that Professor, whose name is inscribed in Horace." Was here when the first case closed. Our firm gave no pianos to any one. Gave none to any one. My name was on the pay-roll of the secret service. Was paid $3 a day. My father got my name there. Col. Whiteley and Mr. Nettleship had pianos, but paid for them. They may have had some influence in getting my name on the pay-roll. They were tried for the safe burglary in Washington. Never heard that these two men were kicked out of office.

Stunning Evidence for the Prosecution.

Maggie Emerich. German servant girl. Live in Tremont Center, Sullivan County, N. Y.; know Mr. and Mrs. Scott. Lived in their family February 7, 1876. Went there February 7, and lived there six days, until February 12. I recognize Mr. Scott; the man who sits beside him (Dunlap) I also recognize; his name is Barton. Saw Scott the day I went there; saw him at breakfast; he came there the evening before. Saw him February 8, at about 9 P. M. Scott, Barton and Connors came to dinner together. Saw Connors Thursday morning. He rang the door-bell; I went to the door and let him in. I knocked on Scott's door and told him Billy was there. Connors went into Scott's room. There was a sudden breaking up of the family. Scott was out this Friday evening. Barton was at home. I saw both some part of the day in the morning; they went out after zinc trunks. Friday, Mrs. Scott came down and asked me to help her pack, as she had trouble about the house and was going to move. I helped her pack to the last moment. Barton was in the room while we were packing; Barton and Scott packed on the floor Barton slept on. Some zinc trunks were brought in; I can't say how many. Scott was not lame that week. I noticed him frequently; I never noticed him lame while I was there. I don't know what Billy did with them. Mrs. Scott engaged me for a month. Mr. Scott had no beard while I was there, only a moustache. He was not there when I went there, but came on Thursday. Connors was a stout man, tall, with a moustache and a burned mark on his cheek; he wore a tall hat, and had a yellow cane. Scott paid the rent when they left, to a man in his room; no lady was there at the time; Miss Ballou was not there; I never saw her; Barton was not sick; I never heard anything of his being sick. There was no cross-examination.

Mrs. Mary McKeever, another German servant girl. I worked for Mr. and Mrs. Scott in the latter part of January and beginning of February, 1876. I have seen Scott and Barton before; I saw Scott the first night I went there, in the dining-room; there was Mr. and Mrs. Scott, Mr. Barton, and Miss Wood. She was there half a day, and went away the day I came, and I stayed there a month and five days. I saw Maggie there the Sunday after I went there. I stayed four days after she came. I didn't stop there. I saw Scott and Barton almost every day. Scott was not lame and Barton was not in ill health. A gentleman named Connors used to call. I used to see him every morning; I never was in the room to hear what they had to say. When he first called he told me to tell Mr. Scott that Billy wanted to see him; he went into the back parlor where they slept; recognize this photograph; that is Mr. Connors; this one is of Mrs. Scott; Mr. Scott only had a moustache at that time. While I was there Scott was home almost every day. I missed him from the house from Saturday night until Wednesday evening, when I let him in. No cross-examination.

Edson, recalled Asked if he ever heard Scott explain why he left his house in 43d street. Said Scott told him on the night of Tuesday following the visit to Springfield with Connors, that had he known as much then as now, he would not have moved, as he was afraid they would find him through the gas office. When he came to pay his bill, however, he found they had his name wrong, and there was no danger.

Detective Pinkerton, recalled. (Shown a letter.) Have you seen this letter before; got it from Mrs. Scott, at her house on Washington Place. She said it was her husband's. (Letter excluded.)

L. B. Williams, recalled. I heard Maggie's description of Connors. Was asked what sort of a looking man Connors was, and the question was ruled out.

Tuesday Afternoon.

Mr. Gillett called attention to the fact that the account book of the Polish music-teacher, who gave Mrs. Scott lessons, does not show that he was at Scott's house at any time in January 1876. Cashier Whittelsey, recalled, testified that at the preliminary examination evidence was given as to Scott's shrug. Serena, the New York coachman, recalled, testified that Miss Rose Ballou rode out with Mr. Scott in the fall of 1874. This was a square contradiction of Miss Ballou, who, being recalled by the defense, denied Serena's statement with great indignation and scorn.

This closed the evidence on both sides, and at half past two Mr. Leonard commenced his argument, speaking two hours and forty-five minutes.

Argument of Hon. N. A. Leonard, of Springfield, for the Defense.

May it please your Honor, and you Gentlemen of the Jury:

None of you can appreciate the reluctance with which I entered into the defense of this suit. I was applied to within twelve working hours of the time that the case was set down for a hearing. I was almost entirely ignorant of the evidence upon the one side and the other, and I confess I had so far imbibed the public prejudice against these unfortunate defendants as to disqualify me for a seat upon that panel. But I was appealed to in behalf oftwo young men who had involved in the hazard of this trial all that was precious for good and hopeful in their lives. They had been deserted by their senior counsel ; they stood convicted at the bar of this court of another great crime, and they were to be tried again by a jury drawn from a community where they thought every man's hand and every man's face was against them. And I should have been false to my own feelings, I should have dishonored the profession to which I belong, if I had not promised that, as far as was in my power, they should have a fair trial and a patient hearing. I thought I could promise in behalf of this court and His Honor who presides over it, and of you who were to fill this panel, that, at least, they should have a fair and impartial trial ; and that your judgment should be a shield, protecting them until, beyond a reasonable doubt, their guilt was established by abundant and by honest testimony.

There is no doubt, gentlemen, that Mr. Whittelsey's house was broken into on the night of the 25th of January, 1876. There is no doubt that the scene which he describes, and which the others describe, as having taken place there, actually occurred. But the government charges upon these two men that they were present and participated in that burglary. Of this they are to satisfy you beyond a reasonable doubt. The degree of proof is to be measured something by the penalty which follows conviction. The penalty is the severest known to our laws, for it is imprisonment for life. This terrible issue is now upon your consciences for decision, and from your judgment there is no appeal. As jurors, as citizens, as Christians, it is your right, it is your duty, to require of the government that they shall prove the truth of their charges beyond a reasonable doubt by adequate, by plain, by abundant testimony, so that there can be no doubt left upon your minds now, or to vex your consciences in the future. Have the government done this ? At the very threshold of the argument I put it to you, as to your first impressions, have the government borne the burden and carried the conviction to your consciences and to you hearts by which you may give a satisfactory verdict in its favor ? The government, gentlemen, have produced here two classes of witnesses. One is the accomplice Edson, and the other comes from the family of Mr. Whittelsey, and a few other stray witnesses that have been pikced up in this and the neighboring county.

I pass by, for the present, the worthless testimony of the worthless Edson, and I shall ask you to consider, in the first place, the testimony that has been produced here by Mr. Whittelsey and his family, by Mr. Holt, by Mr. and Mrs. Crafts, by Mr. Mantor, and one or two others. This crime which we are trying was committed in January, 1876. Thirteen months afterwards, these two prisoners, now at the bar, were arrested. Their arrest was heralded all over the country, by every avenue that popular opinion is reached or public prejudice is made ; and every effort made to fix that prejudice upon these men as the guilty parties. They were brought here to Northampton. Every man, every woman, and every child, of this town, whom curiosity or interest might provoke, were invited to examine them. If they had ever been in this town, either in the day or in the night time, they would have been in their ordinary dress, walking without fear through your streets and entering your shops. Covering over a period of six months that has been mentioned as the preparation for this burglary, and yet, gentlemen, in the whole town of Northampton there was not a man or woman to be found who could say upon his or her conscience that their eyes ever rested upon them before. If there was to be identification from impartial and unconcerned witnesses, it was an entire failure. But it becomes essential to their conviction, and to secure the large reward that was offered for their conviction, that identification should be complete.

It was then determined that Mr. Whittelsey should be brought forward. Mr. Whittelsey, is an honest man, and it was thought that he and his family could complete the work which none other would undertake. Mr. Whittelsey, it was arranged, was to go to the jail for the purpose of identifying these men. He and his family talked it over, and, under the protection and the guide of the officers, they were to go to the jail to identify these men by their voices. They started with no other idea. Mr. and Mrs. Whittelsey, Mrs. Page and Mr. and Mrs. Cutler and the servant, under the guidance of the ever present and ever active Pinkerton, started to the jail with the purpose of identifying these people by their voices. Mr. Whittelsey went with his paper and his pencil in hand, gentlemen. It was pre-ordained that he should identify them. It was written out as his purpose, when he stood with pencil and paper in his hand, that he was to identify them by the words which he was to take down. Of course, they identified them. Why, the whole attempt would have been a failure, the whole scheme would have fallen to the ground, Mr. Whittelsey's paper and Mr. Whittelsey's pencil would have been useless, if he did not recognize them by their voices, because every other plan of identification had failed. But did he do it? Did he do it, gentlemen? He tells you he did. And, gentlemen, Mr. Whittelsey is an upright and conscientious man, and he was not satisfied then, nor do I believe he is satisfied now, that he identified them. He tells you that the first time he did, but he went there again and again. He tells you that he went there the next day and, I think, the day after; and that he went finally for the purpose, as he says, of strengthening his opinion and his statement, because he was not satisfied; that he might listen to them in order to make sure he had identified them, or to quiet the admonitions of his own conscience that he was taking more upon himself than he ought to take. How about Mrs. Whittelsey? She claims to identify their voices. How about Mrs. Page? She comes to you with a woman's reason and with a woman's prejudice, and she says, "I thought and I felt that that was Scott's voice." You see her feelings ran ahead of her judgment. Her judgment followed her feelings, and when she thought that that was Scott's voice, and went there with those feelings in her heart, she could hear no other voice than the one she imagined she heard that night in her room.

Now, gentlemen, let us look a little at this. If Scott was there on the night of January 25th, or if any other man was there and talking to Mr. and Mrs. Whittelsey and Mrs. Page, you may rest assured that they were not addressing them in their ordinary voices. If they came there that night, they were under strong excitement and great passion, and we know that passion and excitement engraft themselves upon, and express themselves in the human voice. They were there with their voices covered up and smothered up under the masks they wore, some of them had mouth-pieces cut in them, and some of them did not. When they heard Scott, they did not know the man that addressed them in his strong passion and in his might on that night of January 25. They heard a man confined in your jail, appealing to the officers for a favor. Hope, if he was guilty, had gone out of his heart. The firmness of his tones had disappeared from his voice, and I tell you, it is preposterous for us to suppose that the strong, passionate voice of the night of January 25, 1876, smothered under the masks, could have been detected in the persuasive, in the imploring, in the subdued, voice that was asking of the officers that held them in prison, for a favor.

Now, how in fact did Mrs. Page feel about these men? We know how Mr. Whittelsey felt. We know that after he assures you that he recognized that voice he went there again and again an unsatisfied man. How did Mrs. Whittelsey and Mrs. Page talk about it in their private conversations at home? Mr. Whittelsey tells you that they were not positive about it; that they were not so positive, and yet Mrs. Page comes here under the pressure and excitement of this trial and tells you that she thinks and feels that is Scott's voice, but in the privacy and confidence of their domestic life at home, they discussed it, and Mrs. Page expressed the doubts which she had. Now, gentlemen, how much does this sort of testimony weigh in your minds? How much weight, in view of the importance which this case is to these two young men, are you going to give to the recollections of the voices spoken under those circumstances and carried in the minds or the fancies of these people for more than a year? And, too, as that voice was in its strong passion, and its smothered tones, repeated as they think it was in the imploring accents of the prisoner in his cell. Try it by your own experience. Put to it the test that my brother Bond gave you last week. Recollect, if you please, those men that came upon the stand for jurymen and were challenged one after another, and tell me if you can remember and discriminate their voices. What sort of a voice has Scott now? You heard him the other day. What sort of a voice has Dunlap now? That you surely remember and carry in your recollection as he challenged the men or admitted them to the panel who are to sit upon his life. Does one of you remember the tones of his voice? Does one of you remember the tones in which he announced his choice of men for this panel last

week, and can you tell what they were, or would you be able to recogni
months afterwards when he should be speaking in the calmness and quie
a right to be able to speak ? Which of you, gentlemen, would know my
would recognize it ? You have heard me here in this court-room, speak i
ment which a trial always produces ? Which of you gentlemen knows my
sational voice, and with what tones I should turn to a man asking fron
venture to say, gentlemen, that to-morrow morning, if I was locked in a
and you were asked to recognize my conversational tone of voice, not
hearing me here in the excitement of this trial, would recognize my o
tional tones ; and would you confirm and corroborate the testimony of F
that Whittelsey and Mrs. Page carried in their ears and their brains eitl
were spoken or the tones of voice in which they were spoken on that fear
But, gentlemen, where are the other witnesses to this identification ?
witnesses who had least to fear, and were most calm on that terrible nigl
the government seeking a fair trial has suppressed them ? Where are Mi
and the servant who had no connection with that bank and no fear of it
government not summoned them here that you may have a real and true
were spoken in their presence ? I have waited, and did wait in the early
for them to produce these witnesses, but not once has the government
there were other witnesses that they might have called, who would give e
to the voices of these men.   They had never admitted to you that there
nesses who had no fear, whose bank was not to be robbed, who lives were
who never once recognized these men, or attempted to recollect their
gentlemen, I know it will be suggested that Mr. and Mrs. Whittelsey an
under intense excitement ; that their whole intellects were stimulated, t
aroused as to be capable of taking hold of and retaining in their memorie
dents that took place on that night as they could not on any other occa
Page tells you that she was unusually calm ; this maiden lady into who
masked man entered at midnight, tells you she was frightened but fo
Whittelsey, who was there being pounded, and punched, and threatene
plaintive cries of his wife, tells you that he was specially on the alert.
how does their evidence prove their calmness, and alertness ? Take i
Whittelsey, who tells you that he was so alert, and he cannot tell you hov
ed.   He cannot tell you what sort of a mask was upon any man's face, n
nor the material, nor whether there were holes for the eyes, or nose, or
all.   Take Mrs. Page, and she cannot, though woman she is, describe
of these people, except, she says, the taller man had on a duster.   Gen
the taller man ?   Her identification, gentlemen, so completely fails, tha
scribe the size and the hight of this next smaller man, and in reply t
says, there may have been a difference in the hight of the next to the
tall man, that there was to the length of that paper, (holding a paper in l
is all she knows.   He was five or six feet high.   And this is the woma
was so aroused, who was so calm and dispassionate, that she cannot tell
the hight of people between five or six feet, how they were dressed,
whether they wore brown or white masks, whether they had a space as b
for the eyes to look through, or none at all, whether they had a place as l
for the mouth to breathe through, or not at all.   I submit to you, gei
testimony of Mr. Whittelsey, and Mr. Whittelsey's family, is utterly wort
is no rule by which it is entitled to any weight here at all ; for, if thes
paralyzed by fear, as I think they were, so paralyzed by fear that they co
the masks or dress of these people, or hight of them, they were far too l
the tone of their voices and carry it in their recollections for a year.
    Now, gentlemen, there is one other phase of this testimony that I tl
consideration.   Mrs. Whittelsey says that she still looked with great in
men, and she marked Scott by the peculiar shrug of his shoulders, and tl
ness of his shoulders.   Mark you, gentlemen, if you please, if the rest o
be believed, Scott that night was dressed with a cap that came tight c
eyes, and nose, with an open place for the mouth, of which they did n
cording to their theory, he was dressed in a loose, brown sack, and they t
was a peculiar shrug of his shoulders and a peculiar form of his shoulder

minutes that he was before Mrs. Whittelsey she saw it and recognized it as a nervous habit by which she expected to identify him in a future time. Gentlemen, here is Scott before you. He has been here a week, and I ask you what is the peculiar roundness and form about his shoulders that distinguishes him from any other six-foot man. Then, she says, there was a peculiar shrug to his shoulders that she saw that night. It was a habit, it was a thing that she marked him by that night. Gentlemen, when Scott was brought into this bar and placed before you, he ran the risk that attaches to habit. He could no more conceal it than I could conceal from you any habit that belongs to me. If it was a nervous habit, he could no more control it than he could the winking of his eyes. He took the risk, and I venture to say that upon this panel there is not a man who has seen the habit shown in him once. I venture to say that the habit alleged has not been found. Mrs. Whittelsey further, gentlemen, says that she not only recognized it on that night, but as soon as he was brought to the bar of the magistrate. I dwell upon this, because it is a test by which you may test them. Because you may apply to Mr. and Mrs. Whittelsey the test which they apply to Scott. It is the only test that is furnished us to test them by ; and the evidence comes here from the lips of by no means willing witnesses, or friendly to the unfortunate people who are before you, and they tell you that in all the time they have been with them and in the time they have guarded over them, in all their attendance at this trial, in all their watching at the jail, they have never noticed that shrug of the shoulders which both Mr. and Mrs. Whittelsey discovered that evening. I say the probabilities are against Mr. and Mrs. Whittelsey's testimony, and I say that when we bring their test into court and look for the marks upon the prisoners which they say were there, they are not to be found, and they never have been found, we then take this testimony to ourselves, and it is ours. For I tell you, gentlemen, that the men that broke into that house that night did have that peculiar roundness of the shoulders, and that peculiar shrug of the shoulders. Where is that man with the nervous hitch which he could not control ? Where is that man that this Edson called Scott, with the shrug that he could not conceal when he wanted to conceal the habit ? Now, if this evidence does not make for the prosecution, it makes for us. It goes further, and certifies that he was not there. We claim it then as our own. We claim it as one of the trial proofs in the case, that the man who was there is not the man who has been arraigned at this bar. I forgot to say, and it is a pity for it that it should escape your recollection, that Mr. Edson says he has a shrug. I do not doubt that Edson knows the man with the shrug of the shoulder. Now, gentlemen, Mr. and Mrs. Whittelsey are very nice people, they are very conscientious and upright people, and would not, for the world, I doubt not, harm these two young men intentionally ; but they have talked this matter over so much, they have sustained and built up each other's belief, they have fortified and concentrated each other's impressions for a fact, that while they mean to be honest and just, they have gone so far as to swear to that which they believe existed, but which never existed. It is not perjury, it is not false swearing, but it is the result of a mental process that we see so often, in which a man comes to believe what he wants to believe. I think, then, with safety we may pass by the testimony of these people. I think we are all convinced that, however good and honest the Whittelseys may be, they cannot furnish us any help against these men. Whatever they have contributed towards the general deliverance, I thank them for, and so far as they have identified the real culprits I am glad of it, but when they attempt to put the stamp upon either of these men, we say they are mistaken, however honest they are.

We come now, gentlemen, to some other outside and confirmatory testimony of Mr. and Mrs. Whittelsey, since that is thought, on the part of the government, to point out these men as the real culprits. There is the testimony of Mr. Holt, of Springfield. Any of you, gentlemen, who know him as well as I know him, might naturally have expected him here. He is a wonderful man to see things, and find things out, and if I was to designate who in this emergency should be summoned here to recognize these people, I should think Holt, of all people, would be first. Mr. Holt sees them under the most peculiar circumstances. Early in the morning they are wandering about Springfield in ulster coats and silk hats, just where the people do most congregate, just in the depot where police officers are most numerous, and just the spot that suspicious characters avoid, he finds and he places these men. I hope you are all acquainted with the city of Springfield. Just below the railroad depot is Hampden street, filled up with wholesale stores, and perhaps next to the Main street, is the busiest street in Springfield, certainly one where the largest wholesale business is done. I think it rather strange, I confess to my mind it appears strange, that these two men, after wandering about the station, should pass down and turn down Hampden street and meet three other strangers, in a great thoroughfare, and hold their conference there about the burglary they were going to commit that night or the next. Why didn't they go to the City Hall ? Why didn't they go where the bank meetings are held ? If any man goes there, he is supposed to be a purchaser, and he is followed like any other trader going into a wholesale street. I am sure in such a place as that at nine or ten o'clock in the morning, rogues do not congregate for the purpose of counselling over a bank robbery, that they propose to commit. And just see how this thing works. The identification is complete. Mr. Holt sees them with ulster coats and silk hats in the morning, and Mrs. Crafts comes to the stand and is equally positive that it is Dunlap dressed in a tight fitting surtout, in the afternoon. Eighteen months afterwards she comes upon the stand and her recollections are as we have learned. Why, gentlemen, do you suppose that those gentlemen were travelling with a large amount of baggage, so that they could make these changes in their clothing ? If Holt saw them in the morning, Mrs. Crafts did not see them in the afternoon, and if Mrs. Crafts did in the afternoon, Holt did not see them in the morning. And, then, I take it that these steady-going, nerveless burglars who commit crime without conscience, and without fear, don't go bobbing from one seat to another in a railway car, making so much noise and fuss as to attract the attention of every traveler. Then there is another identification. It is a funny one. It is very much like the rest, to be sure, but it is a somewhat amusing one, about which the government itself has made some fun and expressed some doubt. Mr. Crafts meets one of these men, and has scarcely any doubt about it, on the 14th day of January, 1876, at nine o'clock in the morning. He met a man dressed in an ulster coat, as he says, near Mr. Whittelsey's house.

Now, if it was Scott or Dunlap, if Edson is an honest man, if Mr. Whittelsey is to be believed, if these men knew anything about Northampton, they knew about the old bank and where Mr. Whittelsey lived. And yet Mr. Crafts tells you that on January 14, at nine o'clock in the morning, he meets a man whom he recognizes as Scott, and Scott asks him where Mr. Whittelsey lives ; asks him what family lives with him ; talks with him right opposite the house at that hour of the morning. I did not wonder that the District Attorney turned to him with surprise, and inquired if it was a fair day, a light day. Why, gentlemen, Mr. Field was surprised himself, out of his self-possession, that a witness should come here and tell you that Scott met him at nine o'clock in the morning, and asked him about Mr. Whittelsey's family and who resided with him. The thing was so preposterous that Mr. Field turned to him and says, was it a light day ? Then, there comes a Mr. Mantor, about whom I know nothing, and about whom it is not necessary that I should say much. All that he can swear to is that he met a couple of men in the early part of February in front of Mr. Whittelsey's house, gesticulating about the house with great violence, " with great movement of the body " as his peculiar and somewhat characteristic expression. Why, gentlemen, it seems that while this man Mantor was approaching, these men did not hear him, and they stood there in front of Mr. Whittelsey's house, gesticulating with great violence and movement of the body, and they waited until he came up and took a full view of them. He thinks he recognizes Scott, he said, but he carried with him no recollection of the other man.

Then we have one other witness, and we are done with that sort of identification, and that is West Sexton, and perhaps his brother. Mr. West Sexton of Springfield, who is clerk in a hotel in the upper part of the city, where two men came on Monday night, leaving the next morning. He came upon the stand, a wonderfully wise young man. He said he looked these people all over. He purposed to impress us with the solemnity and with the strength of his recollection. They had no register, and he looked them all over, and what did he discover ? Not a thing, He said that he could not tell how they were dressed, except he had on a business suit and a heavy overcoat. It was in the month of February, and I would like to know who in that month, would not wear a heavy overcoat, if he had one. That was his identification of the men. He looked them over. He could not tell you the color of their eyes, nor the length of the hair; he could tell you nothing about their persons, except one single thing, that single exception, that in the month of February when there was sleighing, the sharpest month of the year, they wore heavy overcoats.

n, all of these witnesses say that the man who came up here during the
y had no beard. Holt, Mr. Crafts, Mr. Mantor, Mr. Sexton, every one
say that the man whom they saw here in the month of January and
tracted their attention, when they were looking after bank robbers and
ot, had no beard, and it may be true that there was such a man here.
hat there was a tall man with a heavy ulster and a beardless cheek
here in the month of January or February, but that wasn't Scott. It is
such a man was here, with a shrug to his shoulders and a peculiar
ith a moustache upon his face, and without a beard, but that was not
ie other man, and those are the other men we are going to talk about
! it proves anything, if you believe Mr. and Mrs. Whittelsey, if you
if you believe Mr. Crafts, if you believe Mr. Mantor, if you believe Mr.
l you that they have got the wrong man, for the man whom they saw is
igned at your bar. Believe as you please, they have put certain ear-
ey have stamped him with their stamp, they have endowed him with
clothed him with dress, they have painted his picture at their will and
and we bring forward our man, and we place him beside the photograph
d for you, and they are mistaken. Not one or the characteristics which
e men have we here, and as I think I shall prove it before we have
e men whom they saw on the night of the 25th, whom they saw
the morning of the 25th, whom Mrs. Crafts saw in the cars on the
25th, and who was seen on February 14th, have not any of the signs that
; to stamp upon them.
n, I say and I think I am justified in saying, that up to this point there
te failure on the part of the government; that so far as we have pro-
iew of this testimony there has been a woful failure, if these men are
their guilt. Gentlemen, if anything has been done, there has been
own forward to show the innocence of these men in the complete failure
t. The whole strength of the government case, of the government's
esented in this case, comes from the testimony of Edson. There is
!rom beginning to end, unless Edson makes it. And Edson, at the
fies himself as a witness. He says that he was an accomplice, and every
it juror seeking to punish wrong and protect the innocent, demands as
is juryman should demand that a verdict should not be asked of him,
ained by pure and honest testimony. I say Mr. Edson's testimony is
himself is disqualified. The experience of all men and of all courts, is
and lives of the citizens cannot be trusted to the keeping of criminals.
imony and experience of all times and of all men is, that the lives and
tizens cannot safely be trusted into the keeping of the criminals.
: revenge, the love of reward, the fear of punishment, are motives which
fession and the testimony of the hardened criminal; even of the best of
lven of those who have fallen into temptation once, and in moments of
) get back to paths of virtue, the courts tell you their lips are soiled and
orthless, unless it is substantiated and corroborated by honest testimony.
ninals that you and I ever saw, this Edson is the worst and the blackest.
:ommitted great crimes in great passion and excitement, but Edson, at
ie number, in the hardness, in the meanness, in the treachery of his
iassed them all. From his own confession he is a thief, by his own
sion he is a liar. Unblushingly, in the presence of this court
he acknowledges himself the bigamist, who takes on and puts
his pleasure. He cheats his creditors at the rate of ten thousand
, and flees his country, that he might spend their spoils. He dis-
/s his employer, he is treacherous to his friends. Gentlemen, he is the
ie meaner vices. If he is the man he claims to be, if he is the confeder-
he is 50 years of age, and they are young men, and he lead them into
it was that devised the scheme to rob this bank, and he it is that comes
ind stood there testifying against these men. There was no pity in his
) tremor in his voice, as with remorseless revenge, he sought to crush
. I ask you, gentlemen, if from a man as treacherous and crafty, as
norseless, as he is, you will receive the testimony that leads these young

men down to destruction. I ask you as jurymen, if you can pronounce upon the testimony of such a man, that fatal word, that sends these men to condign punishment forever.

Gentlemen, what is the motive of Edson's testimony? what is the inducement that brings him here? He tells you that he did not open his head until these men were arrested. What does it signify? He knew that he was suspected all through New York. He says so, and when the detectives, for some reason or other, put their hands upon Scott and Dunlap, and not until then, Edson steps forward, and says they are the men : under their destruction he could escape punishment, and in their punishment he could have his extended reward. Point to us the men, say the bank officers, tell us their names, and we will give you $25,000. Why, gentlemen, did you ever know, in the court house, in the old county of Hampshire, of a scene like this, that guilty culprit and criminal should confess his crime, without a blush, and come here to escape the punishment which he deserves, and condemn these young men to lasting punishment, and should fill his pockets with dollars and cents, with the hundreds and thousands of dollars that are to be rewarded to the detector of the criminals. I am sure that no jury of Hampshire county ever listened to a like witness stimulated by like motives and like hopes. Now, gentlemen, there is no doubt but that Edson knew what he was about. There is no doubt in my mind but what Edson knows who are the men who entered Mr. Whittelsey's house. I have no doubt that he might go upon this stand, if he had an honest feature in his whole system, and tell you who was that beardless man that came up here and robbed this bank, although I would not believe him, if he did tell us. I have no doubt that all he confesses, all the details with regard to the burglary that he describes, may have been true, but I tell you there is no difficulty in designating any two men that belong to that gang, as Scott and Dunlap. He may call Tom Jones and John Smith, Scott and Dunlap. He may call Green and Thompson, Dunlap and Scott, and every fact that did take place, every word that was spoken, every telegram that was sent, every visit that was made, turns out to be true. True of Green and Thompson, whom he has called Scott and Dunlap. His quick and ready wit, his stony cheek, would carry the rest through. It was a splendid opportunity, that he wanted to escape punishment and obtain his reward, and fall upon his enemies. But, gentlemen, in one thing he fails. In one most remarkable thing he fails ; and when you consider the period of time over which these transactions extended, when you consider that it was from somewhere early in August to January 26, in the accomplishment of this, extending even to February 18, from the discussion of the robbery and the gathering of the securities, it is astonishing that there has not been found one honest, disinterested witness, in the whole world, that has confirmed Edson in one single particular. I say this, gentlemen, inviting your criticism. I say it with deliberation, and I ask you to follow me through the balance of my argument, that so far as corroboration of a fact that fastens and attaches this crime to Scott and Dunlap, there is not an iota of testimony that comes from disinterested witnesses, through the whole trial, confirmatory of Edson. Now, I do not care how far witnesses come forward to corroborate what Edson says Edson did. If Mr. Edson came upon the stand here and said he borrowed keys of Mr. Warriner, and Mr. Warriner said he did, that is no corroboration that affects these defendants. If Edson says he made a plan of the vault of the Third National Bank of Syracuse, and Mr. Gleason is shown the plan, and says it is true, that is no corroboration that affects these defendants. If Edson says he was here examining this bank, and the officers say it is true, if Edson says that he came here by receiving a telegram from Herring & Co., and the bank officers say it is true, if Edson says that he introduced Mr. Williams to Connors, and Mr. Williams says that is true, they don't affect these defendants. Edson may corroborate himself as often as he pleases. He may be like the magician, who turns a somerset and jumps down his own throat. It don't make it true because Edson comes forward and swears to certain facts about which there is no controversy, and Edson is corroborated by the officers of the bank. A corroboration to corroborate Edson, must connect these defendants with him, and with the crime with which they are charged, or it all goes for nothing.

Now, gentlemen, let us take one or two, and I think I am going over all the corroborating circumstances. Certainly, I have not intentionally passed by one, and if I have, I ask my friends here to say so, because I do not want one to escape my observation. Let us, then, begin with the leading one which looks like a corroboration, and that is this Wilkesbarre affair. There is hardly a doubt, in my mind, that at Wilkesbarre, in the

ania, one R. C. Hill did pass from Wednesday to Saturday ; and, I think,
ted that there was a telegraphic dispatch sent to W. L. Edwards, and
s a reply from Hill to Edwards. But, who is R. C. Hill ? Mr. Edson
ap, and without Edson to put his sanction upon it, the whole Wilkes-
for nothing. It may be true that this very man, who has been described
faced man, with a shrug of his shoulders, was at Wilkesbarre. But the
e matter is nothing, without Edson says it happened, and nobody in the
, sustains it. Now, gentlemen, if you are to examine that testimony,
re is against these men, I call your attention to the proof that has been
the government has concealed, as well as what the government has ex-
ednesday until Saturday we know very well this Hill was at the Wyoming
rom Wednesday until Saturday R. C. Hill was at the Wyoming House,
Edson's story, Scott was at some hotel at Pittston ; and yet, from the
House, or from the hotel at Pittston, not a man can be found who iden-
eott as being there at that time. The hotel clerks and the hotel-keep-
women who are in the hotel. Strangers might have been brought here
ng Valley Hotel, or from the Pittston Hotel, and from Wednesday, at
y until Saturday night, these men, according to the testimony of Edson,
not a man can be found from either of these hotels that will confirm one
has said. Where is your corroboration of this ? And, gentlemen, I
on to the absence of corroboration. They brought the telegraph man
d these detectives. They have brought every man here in the United
a that they wanted here. There is no lack of money, there is no lack of
is no tack of means, and if, for a whole week, these men had occupied
ntly for business in these two hotels, I tell you somebody would have
vould have recognized them.
, gentlemen, to the next corroborating circumstance, and that is the per-
published in the newspapers. Edson tells you that he published certain
New York Herald, and he brings the New York Herald to confirm and
Gentlemen, who is Idalia, in the New York Herald ? As you go to your
e these New York personals to read them over, you will find that, in
e are personals that he might have adopted as well as this. There is no-
that puts a corroboration upon it, and Edson says he is a liar. " Knox,
Knox, come home." Knox may have been one of the gang who gath-
lding, at the corner of Broadway and Fulton street, as likely as the man
nox horse. I believe the one as quick as the other. The gang that gath-
House, at the corner of Broadway and Fulton street, was quite as likely
an advertisement of that nature as the man who owned the Knox horse.
e trampling of the grass around the quince bush. Mrs. Whittelsey says
a tumbled, and Edson comes forward and says Scott did it—every time.
nony wanted, there is none to be supplied, but what Edson steps upon
is martial stride, and says Scott. Why, it may be that this other gang
the quince bush and told Edson the story,—this Green and Thompson,
ones, whom he has called Scott and Dunlap ; and Mrs Whittelsey cor-
tions and sanctifies Edson's story. Then there is another bit of corrob-
I do not know how many months,—at least, ever since these poor, unfor-
been arrested,—the government has had in its possession letters, or a
ee of paper on which Scott and Dunlap wrote some directions. Ever
they have had in their possession certain letters, with superscriptions
es, and the admitted piece of writing of Scott and Dunlap. They have
ind out if there was not a resemblance upon the envelopes and upon the
paper. They have searched all Northampton for experts. They have
ld, and have searched all Springfield over for experts, Sometime, I do
but some months ago, Mr. President Edwards took these letters down to
I experts. He applied to Mr. Pinkerton to find experts who would ex-
and try to discover some relation between the standard and the inscrip-
opes. Don't charge them with negligence. Don't believe that the offi-
have left anything undone. Don't believe, gentlemen, they have not
igent. But I tell you that in all their efforts, in all their searches, in all
ot a solitary man could be found until a week last Saturday, when Mr.

Jacob (or Joseph) E. Paine turned up from somewhere. Why, gentlemen, he was over-borne by those absent witnesses before he went upon the stand. He was outweighed by the witnesses they did not call. He was met by an array of witnesses. whom they did not summon, from Northampton, from Springfield, I doubt not, from Boston and from New York, and he was the only man among them that thought, or thought that he thought, they furnished a resemblance. But, gentlemen, he told better than he knew. He gave a true exposition of his philosophy when he said he came upon the stand, not to enlighten the jury, not on the side of truth, but he came to the stand to point out the similarities, and to pass by the dissimilarities, between the standard writing and the envelope writing. What sort of an expert is that that comes upon the stand as an advocate ? What sort of an expert is he who is called here not to help the jury, but to convict the prisoners ? We will put these envelopes and the standard into your hands. We have called here an honest man, born in this county, who has been distinguished by years of study in New York, who comes here and tells that there are similarities, but that there are great dissimilarities There are always similarities to be found where people write, and particularly in a disguised hand, and he tells you that the best of his judgment and honest conviction that he has reached, after a careful examination, is that there is no resemblance between the standard writing and the envelopes. But, gentlemen, you are the judges. The first question is to be left to you. Take these envelopes and this stand-ard to your jury room, search them plainly, search them impartially, and fearlessly, lean-ing on the side of justice and of mercy, and tell me if you find in the statements of Mr. Paine, or in the examination of the letters, the slightest corroboration of his testimony. And, gentlemen, did you know that Mr. Edson appears here again ? I am not looking now at the bulk of his testimony, for I pass it by, but Mr. Edson is again brought upon the stand and he says, I suggested to Scott that he should put those documents, those bonds which were returned to the bank, into the letter. It was a fact which he forgot, at first, to mention. When there is a difficulty to prove these letters he supplies the testi-mony, and says he suggested the thing. And the bank corroborate Mr. Edson by finding the certificates in the bank. I would like to know who is doing it ? Is Edson corrob-orating Warriner, or Warriner Edson ? Then, gentlemen, they find some corroboration, or claim they did, because they traced an acquaintance between Scott and William Con-nors. I know nothing of William Connors, except what appears here. I do not think it is to the credit of these men that they happen to be his acquaintances, but, gentlemen, there is not the slightest proof in the world, except from Edson, that Connors is a bank breaker. He may be one, but I never heard before that the man who stole the money and the securities was the man who carried them back to the owner to sell them. I can easily imagine a gang employing Connors to negotiate for them, but I do not believe that Con-nors, if he broke into a bank, stood his part with the gang, would be the man who met Mr. Williams and talked with him about selling the securities.

We come now, gentlemen, to another piece of testimony. It is the only piece of testi-mony upon which I comment with great reluctance. There is said to have been certain keys found in the carpet-bag belonging to Scott, and certain plans found in the trunk be-longing to Dunlap. Gentlemen, the first question that is raised, is, who found them ? The detectives found them. In both cases, gentlemen, in the bag and in the trunk, the detectives are at work. I know nothing about these detectives, personally. and therefore I have no right to speak about them personally, but I know the detective in the abstract, and I submit to you, gentlemen, he is the nearest in blood to the criminal. From the very necessity of the case, he is his advocate and his companion, and he adopts his mode of life. He is so near, gentlemen, that he sometimes assumes both characters with ease. He be-comes the criminal or the detective, as may best suit his purpose. To be successful, he must adopt the old adage, and "set a rogue to catch a rogue." Gentlemen, you have had some experience about detectives in this county. You have seen how they build up a case ; you saw how they found testimony among the dead or the living, and you saw how the fabric which they built totters and tumbles when the truth is known.

(At this point the court took a recess of five minutes, after which Mr. Leonard con-tinued his argument.)

I say, gentlemen, these detectives were bound to produce a conviction. They say they found the keys in Scott's bag, and they claim that that connects him with a crime which had been committed thirteen months before they found these keys, and having fixed and established Scott's character, as they think, they start to play the same game upon Dun-

d for Scott, is good for Dunlap, and the trick that they had played upon
pon Dunlap. Why, they don't exhibit their ordinary genius and inge-
arrest of Dunlap in Philadelphia, the trunk was opened in New York,
it they call in a New York policeman simply to corroborate and con-
nt. A New York policeman is the highest indorsement that these de-
ploy, at least they say, gentlemen, there were other gentlemen who were
this kind of business, but not one of those five who were present have
They found, they say, the plan in Dunlap's trunk. Why, gentlemen,
which has been played here over and over again. It is Sampson Brass
five-pound note into the lining of Christopher's hat, and discovering it
are about ! Why, this is human nature, says Sampson, is it ? But I
laws of this unhappy country ; forgive me my momentary weakness, it
of his other arm. So, gentlemen, these detectives, like Sampson, per-
le, it is possible, it is a common trick, found in the trunk of Dunlap,
ridence that they want here. I say, gentlemen, the trick is too old. It
repeated to carry conviction to your mind. But, gentlemen, what does
t you to examine it entire, and all the circumstances about that plan
nd it shows how perfectly useless it is for these men to attempt to
It was a plan drawn a year previous. Does it prove that Dunlap and
Whittelsey's house that night of January 26 ? If it does not, it is use-
t tend to prove, to confirm, the story of Edson, that one night later they
uise, breathing out threatening and slaughter to the Whittelsey family?
ve that, or tend to prove it, it is utterly worthless. It was a plan, gen-
: in Syracuse, that had been drawn months before. Now, how did it
trunk ? Nobody knows, at least, nobody tells, and I ask you, gentle-
een connected with a burglary really planned, do you suppose Dunlap
it where he kept his clothes, in his trunk ? That Dunlap would have
ssession a useless plan, that was likely to bring him into trouble ? If it
and Dunlap had put it there, Dunlap knew it, and Dunlap it was that
attention to the fact that his trunk was at the Grand Central Hotel,
hey would not have known where the trunk was, if Dunlap had not told
ure Dunlap would not have told them if he knew there was in the trunk
glar, and the plan of a bank that had been robbed. Give the man credit
What was his purpose in keeping this plan, if he had ever been con-
rime, and why should he ask the detective officers to get his trunk for
a the Grand Central Hotel, in the care of the porter ? And now, gen-
e have the significant fact, that when the trunk was rolled over, it was
Yes, it was found unlocked. When Mr. Rothwell turned that trunk
ilocked trunk. Do you believe, gentlemen, that Dunlap knew there was
ie trunk, that he would not have known it if he had put it there, and
re, do you suppose he would have called the attention of these detectives,
ig him with remorseless fury, to his trunk ? Do you suppose he would
here that trunk was, containing that hidden plan ? And it is strange
entlemen, that they had not sufficient confidence in their own word,
believe they were to be believed by a jury of this county, unless they
y somebody who didn't have anything to gain, or any hope of the reward
reholding out. And so they called in a New York policeman, about this
ut nothing more. When the trunk was opened the first time, Pinkerton
plan, and then went there a second time and took out some wax, which
ere the first time, but did not take, and only took the plan. Wasn't the
rasn't the evidence of the plan enough, that they must repeat the experi-
ie wax ? Do you suppose that this wax, which is so suggestive when
iis crime we are talking of, was found for the first time when they made
here were two things in the bag. There were these keys and the nip-
the detectives' theory. There had been but one thing taken from the
ras the plan, but it gave them an idea, and when they took the wax, and
tion of Mr. Dunlap, I believe I should be very suspicious myself of the
umstances that the government have relied upon.
i, we don't stop there, and we call your attention to the testimony which
night have produced, but have not. I dwell upon this with particular

satisfaction. I charge the government with keeping back testimony, an testimony, that might have been produced in this case. Let me refer to briefly as I may. Edson says that Dunlap and Scott were so in the he his house on Sunday morning and night, that they finally refused to come their habit had been so constant and frequent. Where are the serva opened the door to Scott and Dunlap? Where are the persons that can firm them in their frequent visits?

Not a solitary instance! Neither Edson's wife, nor Edson's children vants, nor Edson's neighbors, nor the policeman whose beat is constantl down by his house. These men were there so often that he says they rei more, and yet not a confirmatory or corroborating witness has been f enough for Edson to swear that he met them at the corner of 50th street up and down the avenue in the night time; that he rode in a carriage w to 12 o'clock, and that these men came to his house so often that they go any more. Tell me, gentleman, where is the servant that opened policeman that trod the street, or the neighbor who looked out of the w of them can be produced here. Where are the crowd on Broadway t who were in the habit of seeing these men go into the Knox building to daily? Not one, not a man. Where are the persons, gentlemen, from the material that has been produced here; the blankets, and iron wor Not a solitary man is to be found. And, gentlemen, I go still farthe attention to one piece of testimony that the government has produced h ton tells you that within two or three days from the robbery, I think as was consulted and on the scent. Gentlemen, on the night of the 6th men started from New York by the New Haven steamboat to go to Sprin ampton. Before the steamboat left the wharf at New York, before she passengers at New Haven, the detectives knew that these men had go horses and a wagon. Thus, gentlemen, as early as the 7th of Februar detective was upon these horses and this wagon, and these men. Be Springfield they knew who they were, and they did not reach Springfield fell upon the very dispatch which was published in the Springfield U February 7:

"Telegrams were received from New York detectives, Saturday, Fe positively that the securities recently stolen from the Northampton Nat buried somewhere in the town, and that the burglars were coming for th

You see they had only just started on Saturday, the detectives kne and knew their mission so well that they described the conveyance th Northampton and how they were going. "The news caused great Now, on Saturday, February 5, the burglars, that entered that bank wc that their movements towards Northampton were understood, and th well that the avenues they were coming through to Northampton wer them. Who were they? They could trace them directly to Hartford ford to Springfield, but, gentlemen, not one single bit of testimony have Edson seen fit to place before us, which was known to them at that dat as early as that, that these burglars were coming to Springfield, why who they were? If they knew as early as that, why don't they bring t here, and tell us who they were, and what sort of a team they drove? tell us where the horses were purchased? And when they got to exchanged their horses from the sleigh, where is the honest hostler th change? And who can identify these men? Where are the men followed them from New York and met them at Springfield, knowing th slow stages with a team? I tell you, gentlemen, there is something w There is something concealed, or something false. The whole theory o is, that two men did come here from New York on Feb. 5th, and the det they were, and what they were to do, and that whole testimony has be kept from you. I ask you if you think they could not tell who Didn't they know on the 5th day of February? Couldn't they have t chosen, when they found out they were coming for the securities? W eighteen months before they summoned that innocent West Sexton fre his hotel to express the opinion that Mr. Scott was the man he looked over c

I would like to hear the suppressed testimony. I want to know what these experts have been about all these months. I want to know why they havn't identified the men whose movements they understood as early as the 5th day of February ? Why didn't they prove that Scott and Dunlap were the men, and not call upon West Sexton to come here and swear to it ? Why didn't they tell you who that beardless man was, with a shrug, and a hitch, and a stoop in his shoulders ? The detectives have not told us all they know. The government has not revealed the whole thing, the most important, the earliest testimony that we have ever heard of, they have hidden from you, and they argue upon the testimony of such men as William D. Edson to convict these men, and send them to perpetual confinement. Do you blame me for not thinking anything of the detectives ? Do you think I was startled here to-day, when I saw those two women come upon the stand, when I knew from the public documents that are published in newspapers, that the most important and conclusive testimony that this whole case has produced, was suppressed, and crowded out, and trampled under foot and concealed, that you might make up an unjust verdict ? These are not the men who came on that steamboat, these are not the men that they telegraphed about ; that they watched at the wharves in New York and New Haven, and warned the men against in Northampton ; it was somebody else, and where are they ? Not one word from the government, not one single bit of explanation of the paragraph in the paper, that is fitted to the whole theory of the government, that these men were known to them. No, gentlemen, the men that are meant are such men as Sexton, as Holt, as Crafts, recognized. I tell you, gentlemen, yesterday the court refused the evidence of a witness, because he would not tell his accomplices in a burglary. I ask you what a Massachusetts jury are going to do with the testimony of detectives who confess they are concealing from you what they know is most important. I ask you if you will put faith in such men, who will trifle, while the lives of men like these are in danger. I ask you if I am to blame when I talk to you about persons actuated by bad motives and the hope of reward, when such a startling piece of concealment of testimony as this is discovered in the case.

Now, gentlemen, I believe I have been over the whole testimony of Edson, and the corroborating circumstances. The testimony of Edson is like a polished shaft. There was no point about it. There is nothing that will attach itself to it, except what he sees fit to attach. There are two points of contradiction. He keeps everything well in hand. What he sees fit to corroborate, he fixes a corroboration, and then, gentlemen, you might as well attempt to attach something by mere adhesion to a piece of polished steel, as to attach anything to Edson's testimony. It stands out as solitary as a liberty pole !

Review of the Testimony for the Defense.

Gentlemen, out of this arena of contradictions, of disputes, of falsehoods, away from the presence of this arch conspirator, and the atmosphere that he breathes and defiles, let us step upon firm ground, where we can breathe pure air and meet honest faces. The testimony that is offered here by the defense, is the testimony to which we invite your scrutiny, with confidence and with pleasure. It is not, gentlemen, what is termed a professional or artificial alibi. It is not the ordinary manufactured article. It was not prepared by contract in the city of New York. It was prepared, so far as we know, under the direction, or rather it is the result of the examination which Mr. Bond gave to it in New York. Into the corruption of the city, something of the simplicity, of the purity, of our country life, went where this testimony was prepared. There is nothing, gentlemen, there is no suggestion of corruption or fraud in the source of it, or in the elements of it, or the purposes of it. It has, gentlemen, the sanction of honest investigation from one of your best citizens, and one of whom you may be proud. Its very imperfection aids its perfection. If it were more perfect, if it were more complete, more positive, we might think that some other hand than Mr. Bond's had guided and riveted it together. and such as it is, gentlemen, imperfect in some details, perfect in others, such as it is, gentlemen, such evidence as it is, coming from old men and young men, from old women and young women, from every variety of classes in New York, which each of these witnesses represents, it is yours—to be presented to you and to enter into your judgment and your mind in making up your verdict. Bear, then, in mind, if you believe it, if you believe any single fact in it ; nay, if it leads you to doubt one single fact in the testimony offered by the government, then the whole fabric which Edson has built up tumbles to the ground.

In this place, gentlemen, the evidence upon the one side or the oth‹
false. Mr. Scott cannot be in two places at one time. Mr. Scott did
and an unshaven face at the same time. It is all true, or it is all false.
in this alibi, one of the witnesses that are called here speaking the truth
that we have attempted to prove, and all this great structure which
here and sustained by the detectives, falls to the ground. The truth ‹
with itself, and believe that there is an honest witness that we have sur
the sanction of your verdict rests upon the defense.

Now, gentlemen, we come to the testimony of these witnesses, ar
young boy, the second was the young girl, and then Mrs. Ballou and Mi
others that we have brought here. They were not witnesses, gentlen
pected to stand the sharpest cross-examination, unless they came tell
would never have ventured to put that ignorant McCue on the stand, u:
fied with the truth, and could stand a cross-examination. We never co
Amelia Wood on the stand, willing to tell all she knew, incapable of
thing, unless she had about her, like a shield, the panoply of truth.
have placed the honest Mr. Nævius upon the stand, who came ther
scholarship of my Brother Gillett, bestowing upon him the complime
us who knew him, know was so well deserved ; we never should have
stand, unless we knew that he was fortified with the consciousness that
truth.

Now, what is it that these witnesses swear to ? They were there—a‹
Pole, whom I had forgotten. They saw Scott through the months of D
and February. Two things they swear to. They swear, all of them, t
beard, and that he was lame. I need not stop to recite the details of t‹
to repeat their names in detail. Every one of them—every one of th
fact, that could escape the notice of none of them that he was lame, an‹
full beard. These two leading facts are the particular and peculiar fac‹
nesses swear to, because those were the things that were at all times op
—the lameness and the full beard. The boy who came upon the stand
way that he did, and would have left it with an error upon his lips, if
corrected by Mr. Gillett ; Amelia Wood, in her simple and almost fligh
Mr. Decker, Mr. Nævius, Mr. Davis, all of them recognized and saw M
months of December, January, February and March, and every one o
positively swears to two leading things of observation, the whole, full be
ness. Now, gentlemen, if he had a full beard, he was not th‹
described and saw, that Mr. Crafts and Mr. Mantor saw, o:
Edson says came to Northampton. Admitting that fact,
is not the man that came here, and when Edson says that ‹
face at that time, then Edson is not only lying about other matters, bu
face in the testimony that he produces, then in order to receive confirn
other witnesses. Take the fact of his lameness, the matter of his lan‹
of these witnesses remembers it, and Decker, by the little circumstance
way when he was putting on the string on the piano ; and Davis has tl
had been carrying. Now, gentlemen, I find some confirmation of this,
parently a bit of contradiction. This man was said to be lame, to b
house, and the fair argument was that if he was lame and confined to h
not have been in Mr. Whittelsey's house on January 25. Now, what do
says he was at his store on the 14th of January. He don't say how
might have rode there in the cars, and he might have got there in son
we have got to deal with the fact that on the 14th of January Decker says
and some of these gentlemen sitting at this table thought there was a
fusion about that. But what does Miss Amelia Wood swear to ? Tha
the 2d day of January ; he was confined to his house a week, and at th
he began to go out a little at a time, from a half hour to an hour, and ‹
gone an hour and two hours at a time. You see the 14th day of Janu‹
a week ; it was two weeks, almost, from the time of the injury, and it ‹
just as Miss Amelia Wood said it did.

Now, gentlemen, we come to other and more confirming testimor
whole month of January Miss Amelia Wood was at the house of her s

that time she swears to you positively that Scott was at home and Dunlap was there also. It covers the whole time, and so far as anything is known positively in this case, Miss Amelia Wood was there during the month of January, and left on the 31st day of January. We have here the simple Pole who tells us he would have been here if he had the money, and says it with significance, that there is not a great deal of money spent on the part of this defense, and that they have not much money to spend in the preparation of this case. We hear of Davis repairing their clothes, and turning the lappels and cutting over garments, and of their practicing and exercising an economy that don't fit very well to Edson's story that they were giving ten thousand dollars for the loan of a thousand. These little domestic scenes, and this insight into their domestic life shows how they were practicing economy in cutting over their clothing, and living with economy, paying for their pianos on installments of ten or twenty dollars a mouth, don't look like the people who are rolling in wealth and breaking and cracking a bank a fortnight. Now I find that this Pole was there through every month on Monday and Thursday. If there had been an alibi prepared, if we had the genuine manufactured article made to order in the city of New York, somehow or other those lessons in music would have been given on Tuesdays and Wednesdays, and covered the precise time that Scott was supposed to be here. But this man, with great honesty, says he was there on Mondays and Thursdays, and Scott was at home every Monday of that month, and that he dined there. It is only significant, because if what this Polish musician says is true, Holt, who says he thinks he saw them in Springfield on the same day is not true. Then we have the testimony of Mr. Decker, who tells you he was there on the 25th of January; that in playing on the piano he broke a string, and he was obliged to mend it on the 26th, because Mrs. Scott took her music lessons on Thursday, the 27th. Now, according to the testimony of Mr. Decker, Mr. Scott was there. He remembers the conversations on the evenings of the 25th and 26th of January, and he remembers that Scott was lame and got in his way while he was trying to mend the string. If this testimony is true, if Decker is to be believed, if he is more trusty than this Edson, then it is the end of the case for the defense. One month afterwards, a few weeks afterwards, he goes to Mrs. and Miss Ballou's, and there he is lame; and on the 18th day of March, on the 20th and 22d, he goes to Mr. Nævius as a student, and Mr. Nævius tells us that among the first things that Scott did when he took his seat in a chair was to ask permission that he might rest his foot in another chair, because his foot was lame. I leave it to you, gentlemen, to say whether that was natural or not; I leave it to you to say whether you think Mr. Nævius was telling a false story to you or not. Take all of these witnesses, gentlemen, who have testified here; some of them have been about here a week, and some of them two weeks. They all testified and answered to their names Friday or Saturday. The detectives have followed them to New York ever since; they have had Saturday and Sunday and Monday to investigate them. The thirty employes of Pinkerton have been at hand, and if anything could be brought against them, if anything could be suggested against them, it would have been produced here. You see how indefatigable these men have been; you see with what diligence they have pushed their inquiries. If there could have been one word said against Amelia Wood or Rosa Ballou; if there could have been one word said against the Pole, whose name I cannot pronounce, or against Decker, or against Nævius, they would have brought it out. Not a word, not a suggestion comes from anybody, unless it is the suggestion of my Brother Gillett, which even the detectives don't dare to confirm or sanction. I leave it to you as gentlemen, I leave it to you as fathers and men, some of whom have daughters at home, whether it was a fair inquiry that my Brother Gillett put to these young women as they came upon this stand and faced this audience; if it was sanctioned by a single bit of testimony that had been offered here or can be put up against them. I leave it to you, gentlemen, if there was anything about them or their evidence that was calculated to carry a stain, and I was glad that the remark which was made was addressed in the presence of jurors who have daughters at home as young, if not as handsome, as she is. I think that some of the reporters who are here to-day, if they review their reports about it, will find I have not suggested anything about Mr. Gillett's cross-examination of them that is not true. But against honesty, against truth, against virtue, the attacks of these detectives utterly fail, and they have come back from New York to-day despairing and powerless against the array of witnesses that we have brought here. Not disarmed, out of the stables and the depths of New York, they have brought one man and two women; one man to impeach Rosa Ballou. He says he remembers seeing her with Scott at the stables some years ago, when Scott was keeping his horse there ; in 1874 he fixes it. And that is all.

Now, gentlemen, weigh this testimony. It is the duty of jurors not simply to hear, but to see the witness, and there they are now ; you see the witnesses before you. They have been in this and the other trial from the beginning to the end, and I ask you to decide the question according to the law and the evidence, according to the preponderance of the testimony, according as it has come before you, to convince you beyond a reasonable doubt. Lay aside all bias and prejudice and weigh this testimony, and tell me the conclusion that it reaches. I say these detectives utterly failed to attack or impeach one of these witnesses, and they have done another thing that confirms and strengthens what my Brother Bond describes this to be, the detectives' case. They came here with two servant girls, with testimony that should have been put in chief of the testimony they had. It was testimony that was intended to connect Scott and Dunlap immediately with the crime. It was testimony calculated to prove that Scott and Dunlap were in league with bank breakers. That they were not in New York, but somewhere else, when the robbery took place. That belonged initially to the testimony in chief ; but when our alibi became invincible ; when our witnesses were found to be honest and could not be disturbed ; when they failed, gentlemen, as all in this court room know they had failed to fix the crime upon these men, they produced two new witnesses, two women, and what is peculiar about it, they simply cover the time from the 26th of January to the 15th of February. Just the precise time ; not a day over and not a day under. From the 23d, somewhere about there, until the 12th of February, these women were where they came from. Who these women were, where they come from, in whose employ they are, and whither they will return, I do not know. But I know it is very strange that two women could be found ; because one was not sufficient, two must be had ; that they were to work in that house, one a week and four days, and the other just ten days. It is peculiar that they were not contented with one ; they had one to confirm the other. They wanted two. What would Maggie do alone if it were not for the other ? You see how it happened that there are two instead of one. Mark you, gentlemen, how quick and how glib this second one swears. She is thinking of what took place over a year ago, two years ago nearly, and as she tells over and over again that Scott was as home all the month of January, over and again she tells that Scott was at home, until she finally remembers that he went away on Saturday night and she opened the door for him on Wednesday morning. How it helps Holt, and Crafts, and the rest of them ! Exactly, she remembers being at the house but a week and four days, how on Saturday she saw Scott go out and on Wednesday come home. Why, gentlemen, if the government had had this testimony, and they profess they had it, they certainly would have put it on the stand.

And so, gentlemen, I have been over all the testimony that I propose to review, and I think I can imagine that you ask why Scott and Dunlap and Mrs. Scott are not put on the stand ? Why are not Scott and Dunlap and Mrs. Scott upon the stand ? I ask you in all seriousness, gentlemen, what good the testimony of these people would be in proving their innocence ? If they are guilty, would they confess it ? If they are innocent, they are to be proved innocent from other lips than theirs. I have been here through this trial, gentlemen, and I knew nothing of it before I came here. I have seen the evidence unfold itself, for the first time, as it has been unfolded to you. I have been reaching out for the truth to know where it lay, endeavoring to discover the real facts in this case, and I have never asked Dunlap and Scott or Mrs. Scott about it. I have never spoken to these men. I never have heard their voices, except when they were challenging the jury. They could add by their word nothing for me, either for or against them. If I am, in my heart to believe that these men are innocent, I should gather no truth of their innocence by what they might protest to me. Do you think I would ask Mrs. Scott if her husband was an innocent or guilty man ? Do you think I would allow her to tell me that she thought they were ? Do you think if I had this conviction brought home to my mind, that I could stand here and look you in the face and charge you as honest men, administering the laws of the Commonwealth, to acquit these people. I tell you, gentlemen, I never yet called a prisoner to the stand. I never have been through the farce, and I could not be here to ask that these men might have their shackles taken off and go upon the stand and declare their innocence to you. Their testimony would be utterly worthless. When Prof. Webster was tried for the murder of Dr. Parkman, his two daughters went upon the stand, and there delivered important testimony. The lawyers for the government asked no questions. They bowed them gracefully from the stand, because they knew that from the lips of those daughters, pleading for the life of their father, no testimony could come that would weigh with the jurors. And so, gentlemen, as I said before, I could not have these men unshackled to protest their innocence to you. They are to be cleared by honest testimony, or not at all. What for us, is of the most concern, is that they have a fair trial. And if they went upon the stand, gentlemen, what could they do but deny the testimony of Edson, that he met them on Lexington avenue and 50th street, or Madison avenue, at Red Leary's, and Fort Hamilton, that they came here? The plea of not guilty covers the whole, and the courts have settled, so great is this right of the prisoner, that a jury are not to draw an inference, because the prisoners don't go upon the stand.

Gentlemen, this has been a fearful fight. The odds of the controversy have been terrible. On the one side, come three young men, confined in prison, without friends, and possibly, I do not know, as their friends could have aided them, if they had called them. On the other, come all the resources of the Commonwealth, that of the capital of the bank, experienced and successful counsel who had been selected against them, with the most diligent, possibly the most unscrupulous, detectives following in their wake. None of us, gentlemen, envy you your position. Look into the faces of these young men. If by your verdict they are never again to see the light of the sun, or the moon, or the stars; if they are never again to look into the faces or hear the voices of those they love; if they are to go into perpetual confinement, from which there is no escape, and where hope cannot enter,—see to it, that your verdict is so free from bias, and prejudice, and doubt; so sustained by the law, and the evidence, that when these men are wasting and dying in gloom and in silence, you may recall it in the future years without fear and without reproach.

At the conclusion of Mr. Leonard's argument, which occupied two hours and forty-five minutes in delivery, and was listened to throughout by a crowded court room with the closest attention, the court adjourned to Wednesday morning, at 9 o'clock, at which time the court room was again densely crowded, to listen to the closing argument by Mr. Gillett.

Argument of Hon. E. B. Gillett, of Westfield, for the Prosecution.

May it please your Honor, and Gentlemen of the Jury:

I come to you this morning in ill health, the result of about two weeks of pretty strenuous labor in these summer heats and in this suffocating room. It will have this advantage to you that, instead of following the minute brief of facts and statistics which I had prepared, I shall address you much more briefly, and I fear much more feebly, than I had hoped to. My Brother Leonard, in his introduction to his very eloquent and consummate argument, suggested to you with what misgivings and with what regrets he entered upon the trial of this case. I am confident that he could not have entered upon his duties with any more of misgivings than I myself did, or with any more of reluctance. But I did not feel at liberty to decline the request that was made to me by the learned District Attorney of this district. This being my native county; this being the county where my father and mother lived and are buried; this being the town where I pursued my professional studies with one of its most distinguished men, and whose name I partly bear, and for myself I have no higher ambition than that I may bring no discredit upon his honored memory. With these facts before me, I could not, in conscience, offer any adequate excuse for declining to render such aid as I could in endeavoring to detect and bring to discovery a gigantic felony, which had thrilled the whole country with alarm. Before entering upon a discussion of the merits of this case, Mr. Foreman, let us clear away a little one or two of the delusions which my brother indulged himself with in his argument, and which seem to have been thrust into prominence before you during the whole of this trial. You would infer from argument, and from testimony, and from endeavor of counsel, not that these two defendants were here on trial, but that William D. Edson was the man whom you are trying. And my learned brother seemed to think that, having denounced him, and having brought him into ignominy, and having announced that "Edson is the whole of this case," and having proved that he was infamous, there was nothing else for the defendants to do.

Mr. Foreman, and gentlemen, I take no issue with the learned gentleman with regard to Mr. Edson. He has said nothing, which, if I should draw his picture, has added one deepening line or damning shade to his photograph. I admit, Mr. Foreman, his villainy. Admit, if you please, for the sake of this trial, that from his boyhood down to to-day his life has been a systematic sinning of the Decalogue through and through, and that he has exhausted the criminal calendar. I admit it all; every word; and if there is any "lower deep" of infamy into which I could plunge him than my brother has placed him, I would gladly offer my aid to explore its depths. But, gentlemen, Edson is not on trial. There are the men that we are to deal with. My learned friend, in his very graceful opening argument of this case, stated to you certain principles of law by which you are to be guided in the investigation of this cause, and he grouped about the prisoners certain legal principles, all of which are true, but stated in language disconnected from the context, convey different rules of law from that which really exist. In the first place, my learned friend suggested to you that you could not convict these prisoners unless they were proved to be guilty beyond a reasonable doubt, and then went on to designate the difference between proofs required in civil and the criminal courts. I agree, gentlemen, that the defendants are to be proved guilty beyond a reasonable doubt. But in every human tribunal it is impossible to arrive at infallible results. In everything appertaining to judicial proceedings we must content ourselves without the aid of demonstration. It is only in the science appertaining to mathematics and physics that processes can be carried on which the result shall be demonstrated beyond the possibility of a doubt. Your doubts, if you have any, must be reasonable doubts, and by that is meant doubts that are well founded; not whimsical doubts; not doubts that any man can create about anything. You remember that there was one of the Apostles who said that "unless I see in his hands the print of the nails, and put my finger into the print of the nails, I will not believe;" and he thereby made his folly immortal, and from that day, and for nineteen hundred years, he has been taunted as the "Doubting Apostle." But it has been urged that every man is presumed to be innocent until he is proved to be guilty, and that this panoply is around him. Agreed. But what is this presumption of innocence? Simply, Mr. Foreman, that it is more probable that a man may not commit a crime than that he will, and that is the whole of it; and that is what this trite maxim of law means. Again, my friend endeavored to impress upon you that these men came here with positively good characters, and a character as good as that of any gentleman upon the panel, or of any counsel in this case. I take issue. I agree, Mr. Foreman, that the law presumes that every man bears a good character; that the law presumes that when criminals are arraigned, charged with a criminal offense, they are innocent of this and every other crime. Therefore the law says that they do stand before you with good characters. But when it is alleged that they have a positive character as good as yours or mine, or my brother's, I deny it. Suppose, Mr. Foreman, you were charged with a crime; suppose circumstances gathered around you pointing to your guilt; suppose you were about to sink beneath the waves of suspicion that were closing over you. What would be done? Your friends and your neighbors would come rallying around you with the testimony of a good and perfect character, the product of a pure and upright life, and would send out this rope into the waves and say to you, "grasp it, and we will bring you to the shore." Any such character here? These, gentlemen, are the legal maxims which the learned counsel has thrown about the prisoners, and which you would suppose furnished an impenetrable panoply, and that these prisoners stood before you like Achilles, with only a single point anywhere, that is vulnerable, through which the shafts of truth could penetrate and touch them. Not at all. The certainty which is necessary to decide that a man is guilty of a crime is the same certainty which is necessary to determine every man in the important transactions of life, and nothing more. You are not, because you are jurymen, in any other condition of mind as to the reception of evidence and as to the reception of truth, than you would be if you were out of the jury box. You bring no other apparatus of faculties to try this case than such as you employ in the most important transactions of everyday life. The rights of man, and the rights of property everywhere, and always, must be determined by probabilities, and that evidence which should satisfy a man's judgment and convictions, when he is at home, in affairs of great moment, touching his own liberty or property, are sufficient for you in the performance of your grave duties here.

Now, gentlemen, with these preliminary suggestions let us proceed to the consideration of some of the facts and features of the case. The evidence against the defendants is two-fold, consisting in the first place of the story of William D. Edson, and consisting, in the second place, of the evidence outside of his story. As has been said by my learned brother, and truly said, the evidence of Edson is to be received with great suspicion and with caution. Here and now I beg leave to say to you that we don't ask you to touch a hair of these prisoners' heads unless it is by other evidence than the testimony of Edson ; unless his story is confirmed and corroborated in many particulars, and important particulars, by corroborating and confirming testimony. And here, gentlemen, let me say that this class of evidence is often indispensible in the investigation of crimes, from the very nature of crime. The government cannot select the style of testimony that it will present to a jury. The government is obliged to accept the best testimony that is presented to it. It cannot choose its agents for the revelation of truth. Burglars and thieves and robbers don't take with them the judges of our courts and the ministers of the gospel, nor the Selectmen of your towns, when they are about to commit some great crime against the community, nor do they make them the recipients of their confidence. No, if they did it would give us great pleasure to present to you a higher class of testimony than we are obliged to employ. Mr. Foreman, suppose that it comes to your experience that five men, not one of whose names or persons you know, should come to your farm or to your home, or to yours, or yours, or yours, gentlemen, and they have stolen your cattle, and mutilated your horses, burned your barns and your houses, and there is no trace of the guilty agents. In the course of time it is developed to you that one of these, perhaps the ringleader and the coward of them all, is ready, under pressure of suspicion or from any other mean motive, to reveal to you who the other parties, his peers in the crime, were ; the authors and perpetrators of the deeds, and whom you had sought for almost hopelessly, and that they were still at large. Do you think, Mr. Foreman, that you would not owe it to yourself, that you would not owe it to the public and to justice, that you should make use of this material that had come to hand. You might bring at least a portion of the men, of these dangerous men who were still preying upon the community, to condign punishment. The great object of judicial inquiry, Mr. Foreman, like all other researches into knowledge, is the ascertaining of truth, ascertainment of truth. And we must go after the truth wherever we can find it, even if it be found "in the bottom of the well," or further down toward perdition itself. And here let me say that truth is not corrupted by the medium through which it passes, any more than light is corrupted which shines upon the unjust as well as the just. The lilies which brighten these inland lakes of ours, are no less immaculate because their roots are in filth. Poison, the deadliest poison, Mr. Foreman, is often a specific remedy in desperate diseases. I am aware that there is a certain sort of sentimentality, developed in our community, now and then, and perhaps in reference to this case, if rumor is to be credited, there have been some weak-minded, imbecile and misled people, who have said "it is a thousand pities that such elegant gentlemen as these should be convicted by the testimony of a scoundrel like Edson," as if the conviction of a felon were not the paramount thing. Why, I infer that it is possible that there are some ladies in this town who almost envy Mrs. Whittelsey the luxury of having enjoyed four hours of intimacy and entertainment with these elegant ruffians ! Mr. Foreman, that sort of sentimentalism is a shame to human nature. They seem to forget that the men who stole Mr. Whittelsey's watch and rifled his pockets of $15, when he had just given them the clew to a million of property, must have been mere "dunghill fowls" in the category of criminals.

Mr. Foreman, let us recur to the testimony of Edson and apply to it some of the ordinary tests of truth, in order to come to a conclusion whether or not his story is true or false. We want to take the whole story ; we want to take the whole fabric of his testimony. And here let me suggest to you that the most wonderful thing about this story of Edson's is this, that it covers such extensive territory, extending from 1872 down to February, down to December, 1876, down to 1877, and during that time and in that story, he has been ready to open to you the whole voluminous diary of his life, and he has challenged these gentlemen to turn it over leaf by leaf down to to-day. He is not endeavoring to fasten a false charge upon these men. He has not selected a narrow and meager circle of facts, and shaped his testimony in reference to that. He has not said, I will pitch on a single occasion and make all surrounding circumstances conform to, and fit in with, that, and upon a time when I know they cannot contradict me.

He has not said, I can put myself with Scott, and I can put myself with Connors, and I can put myself with Dunlap, and name such times and places that contradiction will be impossible. Has that been his policy ? Not at all. He does not entrench himself behind a single narrow rampart, but he exposes the whole line of his movements, extending over a space of years, and invites you to attack him anywhere. Let us see. Let us look and see. Why, gentlemen, I find, in scanning this testimony, that, in between thirty and forty instances, he has named to you different places and different times, giving the exact dates and localities, that he has met Dunlap and Scott and Connors, and Dunlap alone, and Scott alone, and Connors alone, in connection with this conspiracy, which, he says, these men formed with each other and with him, and he has invited them to attack him anywhere, and I ask you with what success have they done it? To run over some of the more important points in his testimony, some of the most salient, we find that he says, in the first place, that a man by the name of Ryan, a livery stable keeper, who lived in New York then, and lives in New York now, giving his place of business then and now, first brought the parties together. Then he goes on and describes what happened then. He goes on and informs you, also, that not long after that he met Scott at Elmira, and that Scott's name was falsely entered upon the register of the hotel, under the pseudonym of Bishop, and he gives the date, and the name of the hotel. He tells that in 1874, Scott and Dunlap robbed the Quincy Bank, and that Connors came and paid over to him what he claimed was his distributive share of the plan. He said that immediately after that, he and Dunlap and Scott and Connors, together, had another interview in reference to that transaction, giving dates and places. He testifies that on July 3, 1874, he was at the National Bank of Syracuse, and at a certain hotel, and that there he made certain plans and diagrams, and that these plans and diagrams he afterwards gave to Dunlap. He testifies that after that, on the 4th day of August, by the request of these men, he came to Northampton, and that, on the 5th day of August, he telegraphed to these parties, at Wilkesbarre, stating that he would be there at a certain time, if he received a request from them. He testified that afterwards he had a telegram from Dunlap, under the name he had given him of R. C. Hill; and mark, while it occurs to me, I may say, if R. C. Hill had no relations to these parties, and they are as ignorant of him as they claim to be, it is quite suggestive and significant that some stranger should have unwittingly employed the initials of Scott's name. "R. C." We find, according to his testimony, that he went to Wilkesbarre, and remained there part of two days. Saw Dunlap. Saw Scott. That they came home. That he gave to Scott the keys which he had received from the Northampton Bank, that Scott might duplicate them for his own use. And we find that after that, in pursuance of that, Scott and Dunlap and Connors were at Northampton off and on during the rest of August, and during September. We find that in September, one Joseph Locke had indicated to Herring & Co. that the lock which was upon the Northampton National Bank was an imperfect lock, and, in consequence of that information, that further proceedings at Northampton were unsafe and suspended. We find that afterwards, at their request, he came to Northampton, and there obtained impressions upon a piece of wax, given to him by Scott, of the keys of the Northampton Bank. We find that they informed him that they had watched Mr. Whittlesey's house, and also watched the movements of the bank, and discovered that the watchman was withdrawn as early as four o'clock in the morning. We find that they made preparations to enter the bank, and that Dunlap and Scott told him on Sunday that they were going to start that night for Northampton, and expected to consummate the robbery on Monday night, but that it was, in some way, interrupted, explaining to you just how it happened that these men were seen at Springfield on Monday and Tuesday. Then we find that on the 26th day of January Edson was at Bristol, and that there he received a telegram from Herring. Herring's books confirm him, showing that he was not there the day before. Then you will remember that on the Sunday morning afterwards a "personal" was put into the New York Herald as Edson tells us: "Idalia, G. Monday evening, 6 sharp; very important." He says that in consequence of the "personal," which had been agreed upon by him and Connors and Dunlap and Scott, he met Connors, and Connors paid over to him some $1200 of money of the Northampton Bank, in new fives and in precisely the same bills which Mr. Warriner testified that they had just then, for the first time, begun the issue. This was on the 30th. We find that afterwards, on the 7th day of February, and that was Monday, Edson meets Connors and inquires of him with regard to Scott and Dunlap, and Connors informs him that Scott and Dunlap have gone to Northampton after the property. We find that on the very next day there is placed in the Herald, and Edson says that he then admonished Connors that Northampton is on the alert, and that it is not safe for these men to go on for the property. Then he tells us that, by Connors' re-

other "personal" into the Herald, " Knox, come home," and that
n that Scott will understand that, because " Knox " was the name of
wned, and that Connors himself goes on to intercept him. We find
wo after he meets Dunlap, at a place named, and inquires of him
s returned, and he learns that he has not. The succeeding day he
Scott informs him that he went to Springfield and returned without
npton, and that they did not return (a fact a little extraordinary if
cated by Edson) in consequence of the advertisement, and that they
inors. On Friday he informs us that he met Scott, who explained
turned. We find that after that, on a certain day and place named,
at the property is returned, and of the exact day it was brought
ty the 13th, it was arranged between the parties that Edson should
ank officers and endeavor to negotiate profitable terms for the re-
rty. On Feb. 18th he informs Scott and Dunlap of the result of the
urges them to close the arrangement at once. They then apprise
ve now got the property into their own possession and should ne-
ess in their own and usual way, and intimated to him that they can
further services in the matter. He does not meet them again until
September. He demands explanation—is denounced as having
ile party, which he denies, and is told that they do not propose to
ied cent." The witness then describes subsequent interviews, giving
es, places and parties. Now, gentlemen, I confidently submit that
t have recited to you such a multiplicity of facts, stated so circum-
ng so much space, and time, involving so many details, and reckless-
ielf to contradictions, upon any other hypothesis than that he was
s and knew that his story was true. The story bears unmistakably
ence of verity. Isn't it so?
s far, Mr. Foreman, only referred to the story itself as bearing in-
ruth. Now is introduced the other questions whether or not Edson
ind confirmed in important particulars in this amazing story. Per-
estion you would ask, is this, however. What motive has Edson
has he had, at any time, in telling anything but the whole truth in
iy that he could have had no other motive. That was his only
' ground he could stand upon, or tread upon securely, was that when
hing he should confess the whole and the exact truth. In the
has been referred to already, of the Commonwealth against Knapp,
arked :—
ie, the moment an accomplice is permitted by the Attorney General
ure, he is safe; he is beyond hope or fear; his security is as com-
received a pardon. The only thing which can bring him into
arture from the truth."
en, in this case it has been suggested that Mr. Edson is a bright and
His mind is a "polished column," my brother tells us. He is a
ar, acute insight and apprehension, he is a man who knows what he
knew that the only safe thing for him to do was to tell the truth. If
iromise of pardon, any promise of relief, any promise of security, it
he condition of telling the whole truth. What possible motive could
My brother suggested, you know, in his opening that they expected
old the truth in the main, but that he substituted other parties for
t. What object was there for that? What was he to gain by leaving out
fraud, when he must have known with this vigilant detective force, all
is falsehood must, at once, be revealed and he himself arrested? Not
e select two such men as Scott and Dunlap, as the subjects he was to
e Northampton bank, as the perpetrators of this crime. Why, gen-
men, with their bevy of confederates about them, his life would not
iur, and he knew it, and he knew that the only way for him to acquire
hese men, the only way in which he was safe, was to demonstrate to
i-conspirators by his testimony that they were in his power, to show
his power, that Dunlap was in his power, and that Connors was in
life would not have been worth a farthing. How long would

his life have weighed in the balance against these men, and how muc
as the weight of the feather of a humming-bird's wing. No, he adop
and safe course, the only possible course that was left open to l
bosom and make a clean and complete revelation; and therefore it
to that stand and challenged investigation and invited scrutiny ; and
theory you don't believe that he could have dared to open his mouth
to have invited and challenged scrutiny. Therefore, I say to you, t
of Edson, alone, of itself, without any corroboration or confirmatioı
or from any source, bears upon itself the image and the superscripı
But, gentlemen, we go a great deal further. We say that he is confiı
orated in a great variety of important particulars. In the first place
corroborated by what happened at Wilkesbarre. Edson says that wl
ton he sent a telegram to Dunlap under the name of R. C. Hill. W
it. You remember what that telegram was, and it is not necessary :
it. We show to you that the telegram which he sent from Northar
barre, was received by somebody. We find by going to Wilkesbarı
the hotel register, that the name of Edson and R. C. Hill are recordı
son of these signatures with Dunlap's handwriting, we find that R.
the register and on the pass-book of the telegraph company, were
lap. We have exhibited the telegram he sent by previous arrangem
son, under the assumed name of Edwards, and that also in his handwı
the words, "come to-morrow." The comparison of the handwriti
and it requires no expert to show you that Edson's right hand wrote
hotel register, acknowledged the receipt of Edson's telegraph, and
in reply. In this history at Wilkesbarre, we have a most striking ar
roboration of Edson's story.

There is another important corroboration to which I have already
to the occasion when, after being informed by Connors that Scott w
Northampton, for the property, and that Connors, upon being info
terprise was unsafe, himself offered to go to Springfield, and that he
place in order to warn Scott that it was unsafe to seize upon the sp
And we found from the testimony of Sexton, that at the time when E
sent Connors to Springfield, Scott himself was there, on that very
team such as Connors described. That after Scott had departed, a
can have no doubt was Connors, came to Sexton and inquired of h
men. And then, that upon inquiring of Scott ofter he returned, whe
nors there, Scott told him that he did not see him, and that he came
sequence of the notice Connors gave him, or the "personal " in the
he came away from other causes, which I shall explain to you by anı
say, he is confirmed in this.

He testifies he was in Syracuse on the third day of July, and at th
a craft of the Third National Bank of Syracuse, and that he gave tl
lap. Is he confirmed in that, Mr. Foreman and gentlemen? We
president of the bank, and he says that on the third day of July, Edsı
says that he was around the bank for five or six hours We showed
which Edson says he gave to Dunlap as being the diagram whi
tion of the bank, and he identifies it as an accurate description of tl
we go further, and this document which Edson says he gavı
find in Dunlap's trunk, under Dunlap's lock and key. How
for that? No confirmation? My Brother Leonard yesterday
of plausibility that had a vast deal of fancy and a slight bas
endeavored to explain to you that fatal piece of testimony aboul
trunk he claimed had been broken open before that document waı
Not at all. When was that trunk broken open? My Brother Leonaı
that Mr. Pinkerton had no key to that trunk until Dunlap gave him
he did not examine the trunk until these suspicious articles had bee
his connivance. Not at all, not a bit of it. Mr. Pinkerton swears
Scott were arrested in Philadelphia, with their burglar tools, on the
ruary, and that by telegraph he heard of it, and on that same dr
Grand Central Hotel and broke open the trunk himself, in the pres

tel, and of the porter, and then he took away from that trunk the dia-
rds, he says he took certain other articles, and left it then in the care
· of the hotel, and afterwards, he says Dunlap sent down, as he states,
away these evidences of his guilt, and the proprietor of the ·hotel
hem up, and Dunlap tells Pinkerton·that the proprietor of the hotel
nder them, and asks him to go and get them, and then he goes and
ink. Then it was he took away the photographs of Connors and Mrs.
iece of wax, precisely the same sort of a thing that Scott gave Edson
his quiet impression of the keys of Mr. Whittelsey's bank. That is the
n intimated to you that these detectives are not men that you can trust.
ouse of Pinkerton is no stranger in this country. You have heard of it
ain, that when the commercial and the municipal detectives failed
these honest men were resorted to. An old house, which has been in
orty years, founded by that man's father, an honest Scotchman, who
isiness to-day. Do you remember the Mollie Maguire outrages in
Ask the honest citizens of Schuylkill, who had been shadowed for
ers, and who lifted up their hands with benedictions on the Pinker-
last they had brought the miscreants to light, and that, too, through
imple. And from that time to this, through their instrumentality
id order there has reigned there as before. These insinuations and asper-
njust, and it is not safe to suggest to a jury that Mr. Pinkerton was
: and fraudulent placing of this piece of testimony in Dunlap's trunk.
that Edson is confirmed and corroborated most conclusively by the
ng out of the diagram of the bank in Syracuse.
another piece of testimony by which he is confirmed. It appears by
at here was a conspiracy in which Connors and Dunlap and Edson
ie parties. Connors, according to Edson's story, was designated as
uld negotiate the securities, and Edson tells you that Connors did
thampton; the others did, and Connors was to stay behind and ne-
ler. Edson says that after that, along in the fall, he tried to make
which these securities should be negotiated and placed again in the
k, by means of the bank paying a certain sum for them, and that he
with Scott and Dunlap, and Leary was present on that occasion.
rerge a moment and allude to another fact, which I might mention
sons or motives that actuated Edson in what he did. We find, ac-
1's story, that early after the loss of the property by the bank, he had
1 Mr Williams, and the defendants confirm the fact, and that from
eavored to have the securities negotiated back to the bank before
emoved from Northampton. That was his object and interest, be-
e that if he could arrange to negotiate the securities with the direct-
.t Northampton before they left Northampton, and a certain sum of
: arranged for, he would know precisely how much the sum was, and
: sure to have his fair share of the plunder, and then he would not be
vas in the Quincy affair. And that is just the reason why Scott and
ot negotiate them, and that is the reason why they insisted upon
ing brought from Northampton, in order that they could "beat"
atter, just as he was beaten in the Quincy matter. Edson knew
ad gone on to Northampton, and he knew that their purpose was
e securities, and he was determined to stop it, and sent Connors
is notice of "Idalia;" and the question will perhaps arise whether or
ie means of sending on to Springfield or Northampton, the materials
notice should be made, which appeared in the Springfield Union
:b. 7th, 1876, viz: "Telegrams state that the securities are buried
e town of Northampton, and that the burglars were coming for
u can see that Edson had a motive in all this matter, and you can see
motive that is disclosed. We find that he tries to arrange for the
e securities. He finds that he cannot do it. They thwart his efforts,
finally telling him he shall not have a "damned cent," and is sold
is, and not till they thus betrayed him, that he takes the matter into
nd at last makes a full disclosure. And now, gentlemen, let us recur

again to the matters of corroboration growing out of that fact. I say, it was understood between Connors, Dunlap, Edson and Scott, that Connors was to be the negotiator. According to Edson's story, they had a conference together, and it was arranged between them that Edson should be the medium by which communication
should be made between the Northampton Bank and the burglars, through their
special negotiator, Connors. And what does he do? Edson says, that immediately
after that was agreed upon and arranged for, he telegraphed to Mr. Williams to come
on to New York, and in pursuance of the arrangement made for that purpose: that
Williams came to New York, and that he agreed with him that he should have an
interview with Connors. Mr. Williams corroborates him entirely. He comes to the
stand and swears that in accordance with the arrangement made between him and
Edson, he went to Connors' place, had an interview with him there of two or three
hours, in a vain endeavor to get back the securities, and that afterwards Connors
met him at the Windsor Hotel, and that after that he and Connors conferred together
for an hour in Central Park. Is that no confirmation of Edson? Is there any explanation other than in the entire truth of Edson's version of the facts, and that
Connors and Williams had that interview in consequence of and in pursuance of the
arrangement claimed by Edson to have been made between him and Connors and
the defendants? I submitted, a few moments since, that the testimony of Edson,
from its palpable, intrinsic truth, from its internal evidence, was such as to entitle it
to your credence. Now I ask you if, taking that evidence, reinforced as it is by these
corroborative facts and circumstances, not one of which can it be pretended that Edson created, the conclusion is not irresistible, and does not the testimony seize upon
and grapple the defendants inextricably?

Now, gentlemen, we come to another class of testimony which is independent of
Edson, and at the same time corroborative of his history of the case. And I refer
now to the chapter of events which occurred at the house of Mr. Whittelsey. It
seems that on the 26th of January, 1876, while Mr. Whittelsey and his family, shield-
ed by the law, as they supposed, were asleep beneath their own roof, their house was
entered by five men. The outer key was turned by these nippers. Having once
entered the house, they silently passed up the front stairway, and with huge sledge
hammers broke down the doors and entered the sleeping rooms of the inmates. We
say that two of the parties engaged in that enterprise were Scott and Dunlap. We
don't assume to identify any of the others, but we do identify those as being the leaders and the chief actors in that brutal midnight drama. We prove it by Mr. Whittelsey, by Mrs. Whittelsey, by Mrs. Page, three witnesses of large intelligence and
high character. They swear, according to their best knowledge and belief, these are
the men, and they are confident in their knowledge and belief. Mr. Whittelsey testifies with confidence. He recognizes Scott chiefly by his voice. He states how much
conversation he had with him, and how frequently he heard his voice during those
long four hours, and his opportunities for accurate observation. He was at special
painstaking in listening to what was said, and in scrutinizing what was done, and even
their manner and bearing were marked with special reference to identification there-
after, and noticed the peculiar shrug of the shoulders which we have proved was characteristic of his bodily motions. Mrs. Page testifies that she identifies them by the voice
and bearing and from a variety of characteristic facts. She says: "I thought, at the time,
if I should ever meet them again I should know them." She has now met them and does
know them. Mrs. Whittelsey as positively and for like reasons recognizes them.
They all have no hesitation in declaring to you that these are the men. My Brother
Leonard scouts the theory that the voice furnishes any adequate test of identity, and
asks how many would recognize the tones of his voice if they should hear it to-morrow? Very true. The breath of human eloquence passes away from the public
assembly and leaves no trace. That is not this case. You are to take the circumstances in which these persons were placed. Here I refer to the suggestions I submitted in a former investigation of these facts, as reasons why these persons should
remember. Their faculties were edged and sharpened by the excitement of the hour,
so that they are able to remember and recall precisely the tones of the voice. Here
they were in their own home, with five masked burglars surrounding them, conscious
that their purpose was the commission of a great felony, part of the time bound hand
and foot, part of the time sitting side by side with these men, marking every tone

and movement, their minds were excited, their minds were on the alert, their minds were quite like the plate in the camera-obscura which when it is ready to receive the impression and the image falls upon it, receives it in an instant and it is made indelible; and is the human eye a clumsier invention than human contrivances? They say they remember the tones of the voice. So Mr. Whittelsey says, so Mrs. Page says. And that is one of the methods in which the mind takes in impressions, and these are made instruments of proof in legal investigations. In the case of Halligan and Dailey, who were executed in Hampshire county, the voice was the mode of identification. Why, even the old patriarch Isaac was deceived in his sense of touch, but he recognized the voice of Jacob. So it is in many and many a case cited from the books.

(Here Mr. Gillett referred to instances recorded in the State trials of England, which he cited in his former argument.)

Do we not all know, Mr. Foreman, that our senses are quickened and intensified under strong excitement? It applies even to our grosser faculties. That mother who lifted with ease the timber which imprisoned the body of her child, but which required two strong men to replace, illustrates the theory. But my Brother Leonard says Mrs. Page says she was never more composed in her life; never more cool! Cool! Cool as the engine is cool when under pressure it is ready to do its work. Cool as Napoleon was cool when, sitting in his saddle in the midst of the smoke and thunder of the fight, he could maneuver forty thousand troops, ranged over miles of territory, so that he could summon division after division, column after column, and concentrate them at a single point at the same instant, and thus perform, as he said, mathematical problems by intuition, which, in the quiet of his tent, would have required hours of calculation. It is such a coolness and composure that these men and women had on that fearful night, and the impressions were seared upon their eyeballs, and they retain them at this hour. And when they stood there and confronted these men, it was with absolute confidence that they exclaimed, These are the men!

But, gentlemen, we don't rest here. This striking testimony, so confirmatory of Edson, is itself corroborative. Is there other evidence tending to show that these defendants had been in Northampton about that time? My Brother Leonard made himself merry, somewhat, over Mr. Crafts' testimony. All that Mr. Crafts testified to—I suppose he is a respectable citizen of this town—and he informs that on an occasion, two or three days before the robbery, he saw a man near Mr. Whittelsey's house, looking intently toward it. That he had Connors with him; that he asked him if that was Mr. Whittelsey's house. Brother Leonard seems to think that was very strange. Not at all. The man was probably looking at the house with an intenseness that required an explanation, and so, in order to carelessly relieve suspicion, he did the most natural thing in the world, he asked where Mr. Whittelsey lived, and if he did not do that Mr. Crafts gives a further clue to the conversation, when he said in reply to something Scott asked him, he informed Scott that there was another family in the house. This was important information to Scott. But Mr. Crafts does not say, I saw a man there, and I recognize him to-day, but he testifies that after, on the Saturday before the burglary, he was standing in a grocery store in this town, and that then and there he saw the same man, and the mental process passed through his mind that this is the same man that I met upon the street the other day in front of Mr. Whittelsey's house; and then he goes upon the stand and says to the best of his belief that Scott is the man. Then there is the similar testimony of Mr. Mantor, applying to two occasions, and it is of the same sort, confirmatory entirely. So much for Northampton. But, gentlemen, there is no testimony in this vicinity that clusters about these defendants so clearly, and with such connecting power, as the occurrences at Springfield. We find that on Monday morning before the robbery, a well-known citizen of Springfield saw these men. Mr. Holt tells you that he went to his office in the morning about eight o'clock, and he saw these two men as they crossed the street opposite to him. He saw them go down to the depot; afterwards he saw them on a side street, which my Brother Leonard talks about as being a wholesale street of business. Possibly a wholesale liquor-dealers' street; a place eminently fit for burglars and thieves to congregate upon, and there he sees two men meet three other men coming from an opposite direction, and they have a conference together. Then, afterwards, he says he saw them again that day, and saw

the five men meet again and confer together. He saw them the nex
rate and grouped, and called the attention of another to them.   Nov
question was asked of him whether or not these were the men, and
was positive about it, and that he had no doubt that Scott and C
persons.

My Brother Leonard made a remark with reference to Mr. Holt,
think he would make in his presence or the presence of his friends,
he should think Mr. Holt was just such a man as would see them, a
expect to see them and identify them.   If he said it ironically, and
his tones indicated, then he conveyed a wrong impression of Mr.
men in the city of Springfield who would accurately and infallibly c
such men, it would be Mr. Holt.   His high character is unquestione
who has been recognized in the city government of Springfield over
in positions of trust, and more than that, according to his own test
for eighteen years paymaster of the Boston and Albany railroad, pa:
forty thousand dollars a month.   Having had this business on his h:
would naturally sharpen his eyesight and faculty of observation, s
know his men, that when employes came in for their pay he s
whether they are men who have been there before, or whether they a
palm themselves off for employes, a trick formerly not unfrequent
of his carrying large sums of money from one point to another, he
senses, and when he saw these suspicious persons, he stamped them,
and he remembered them, and had pitched upon them when he firs
crowd, and he knows that these are the men, and so swears to you.
robbers?   They were at Springfield, and you will infer, of course,
not come into this town, which was to be the scene of their plunde
day.   They would not come.   They would naturally feel comparativ
against which they had no evil designs, and would be careless of e:
fact that they were there two days is explained by Edson, when he s:
told him on Sunday that they intended to make the charge on the
night   It seems that for some reason they were detained in Springf
than they intended.   But this is not all.   There are certain other m:
which have been introduced into the case.   We find at the house of
piece of wrapping paper bearing the name of Hall & Prew as clo
Springfield.   Mr. Hall is called upon the stand and identifies a pa
being such drawers as he sold in Springfield, a day or two before t
although he cannot identify these men as the men, he remembers tha
at some time, he has seen them.   And then we find in Mr. Whittel
garment, and we find it fitting like that, and we find from the testim
a portion of this garment was worn as a mask, in Mr. Whittelsey's h
So we have all these facts of corroboration.   And, gentlemen of the
to all this, we have introduced another piece of testimony which see
ially significant and worthy of your consideration, and that is cert
introduced to you a receipt, which is confessedly in the handwriting
we introduce to you a gentleman from New York, of A. A. Low &
know anything of these gentlemen, you know that for wealth and m
iness, and respectability of character, there is no superior in the cou
partment.   Mr. Lyman, formerly of this town, and he has a summe:
now, being a member of the firm.   We called Mr. Joseph Paine, :
upon the pressure of counsel upon the other side, and if anybody
own capacity I suppose he does, and according to his best judgment h
worth are probably the only competent and accomplished profess
handwriting in this country.   Now he has compared their writings :
his judgment upon them, and he gives you as his unqalified convic:
that the hand which wrote the receipt wrote these letters and super
ters, and when you look at their contents you will know, that who
letters are the burglars of this bank.   Perhaps it is of very little
by reading them you will find that if Scott wrote those letters, any
was making precisely the same complaint to the bank that he had
Edson.   He says that somebody is trying to negotiate with you who

to negotiate, and he says somebody is trying to negotiate with you who is "standing at both ends." Do you recollect that? "Somebody is trying to negotiate with you who is standing at both ends." Who was that somebody? Who was the man that was writing to them warning them not to negotiate with the man who was standing at both ends? Edson was the man, as appears by Mr. Williams' evidence, who was standing at the bank end, and Edson was the man that the writer referred to when he warned them that it was idle for them to endeavor to negotiate with any other party, and if they wanted to negotiate they might negotiate with the writer, and to prove his genuineness, he enclosed in the letter two of the stolen certificates. Mr. Foreman, Scott wrote that letter, and nobody else could have written it. So much for that testimony.

(At this point the court took a recess of five minutes, after which Mr. Gillett resumed his argument.)

Gentlemen, I have at a great deal more length than I expected to, taxed your patience in considering the testimony claimed by the Government as conclusive of the guilt of the defendants. We say that this testimony is not to be judged of as each piece stands alone and fragmentary. It is not that unsupported single column, such as my brother alluded to, with nothing to support it from beneath, and nothing to grapple it from above, and nothing to lean upon on either side; but it is testimony reinforced and stabilitated in most significant and manifold ways. Each piece is surrounded by its corroborative and confirming facts. And you are not to take each piece by itself. Of course you will examine the entire fabric of evidence. You will examine it as you test the strength of a cable which holds fast the ship at anchor. Take it strand by strand, and fibre by fibre, and you can snap it with your finger, but braid them together and then try it! And I ask you to look at the remarkable combination of testimony, in order that you may get the full force and effect of it. Taking it singly and standing alone, you may say that each piece of itself is not conclusive. But that is not the way to look at it. You might just as well analyze a single drop of water in this glass, in order to discover the power and majesty of the ocean, as it comes breaking in thunders upon the shore. But take this testimony together, in its aggregation and accumulation, and I submit there is no withstanding its force, and that all the testimony which has been introduced on the part of the defense is as tow before the fire. Now, gentlemen, let us inquire what has been the theory of the defense? Its chief aim has been to prove an alibi, to prove that these parties were not there. And, of course, if they were not there, and you are satisfied that they were not, then that ends the government's case. But, I suppose there is nothing more unsatisfactory than the testimony which is denominated an alibi, as gotten up by the party of the defense in a criminal case. Tonly Weller only voiced the sentiment which has been going on for generations, when he asked of his hopeful son, after the trial was over, "Oh, Sammy, Sammy, vy worn't there a alliby?" and that, too, in a breach of promise case! Gentlemen, that is the easy resort of persons who intend to manufacture a defense. My Brother Leonard alluded to the Webster trial, in the course of his argument. They had five intelligent witnesses, men and women, who swore to seeing Dr. Parkman in full health and moving in the streets of Boston, when by Prof. Webster's own confession, afterwards, the body of Dr. Parkman had already been mutilated into fragments, and at that very hour was hanging piecemeal on fish-hooks in the vault of the Medical College, or was part decaying beneath the action of acids, or consuming in the fires of his furnace. No. But let us look a little at the testimony upon which they rely. And, in the first place, I refer to the testimony of Pstrokonsky, and let us see how untrustworthy that testimony is. What was their alibi? What was its theory? It was that in January and February Scott was elsewhere, and Dunlap was elsewhere, and Scott, beyond that, Scott was lame; that he had sprained his foot early in January, and continued lame certainly down to the 22d of March, when he was receiving instruction from the Professor who was so fresh from his classics. And if he was not any more accurate in his facts than he was in his classics, I do not wonder that my Brother Leonard smiled. I presume because he, always fresh from the classics, discovered that the erudite professor misquoted the Latin and mispronounced the English. But what do they attempt to prove by these persons? They prove that he was absent and that he was lame. And the first piece of testimony that they introduce here is from this music teacher, and the question that they

ask him is this. Perhaps it is hardly worth while to go over the dep
inquire of him where he was in the month of January, in reference to M
and he testified that during the month of January he gave lessons to M
every Monday and every Thursday. Then, upon cross-examination,
of as to his means of information, how he happened to be so accurate
to his memorandum book as one of the special sources of his informat
member that. And then, gentlemen, we look at his memorandum boc
you will find upon referring to it, Mrs. Scott's name mentioned in a :
count, the grouping of all his professional visits. And you will obs
count commences the 5th day of January, goes on to July, August
October, but December and January are nowhere mentioned. Ther
nothing to indicate that he was there, in a single instance, in the m
There is nothing to indicate that he was at Scott's house during the
he further adds, that he took dinner there uniformly, when he gave
he gave his lessons at twelve o'clock, and yet, according to the G
were servants there, they dined at three or four o'clock, invariably
testimony is concerned, we say it is worthless; it is not worth so m
smoke from the cigars peddled by his wife from her cigar stand. .
you will mark that this testimony was taken on the 20th of last Jun
You will find also that the deposition of Mrs. Ballou was also take
and you will find that the testimony of Mr. Raphael, if that is his
last June. And here is this music teacher, who was there twice a v
fied, during the whole of January, as also in February, and Mrs. Bal
same means of information that her daughter had, and Mr. Raphael, v
rent, and not a single question is asked of Mrs. Ballou, or the n
Raphael, whether they noticed that Scott was lame. That question
then never occurred to them; it was an after-thought! My Brother I
that here is an alibi which is very imperfect, but very true, and true I
perfect and not gotten up by artifice—and intimates that it was prep
cellent Brother Bond, and who he suspects may have gone down to
that purpose, and how refreshing it must have been to have seen
gentlemen in that great and wicked city! You would infer that th
Brother Bond in New York was like a breath of fresh air from our
the murmur of a country brook. Not much, Mr. Foreman! Besides
ing to do with the fabrication of this alibi. We discover that here
lawyer, More, who was here day after day during the first trial, and
and forth between this town and New York during the present tria
paring and supervising the alibi. Yet, from all these depositions an
June last, not a word or syllable about Scott's lameness, but now by
on the stand, they extend this lameness from the 2d of January dov
March, when with the gentle professor as a student. And the prof
reply was very significant. "Did you notice his lameness then?" n
inquires. "Why, yes, because Mr. Scott called my attention to it b
sion to place his foot upon a chair, in order that he might rest it fro
Undoubtedly so! The good professor thought that he was training
matics and the languages, and the fine arts, but Scott knew that he
professor for a witness! There is the story. Now I do not propos
with the various issues of testimony which they have introduced, I
fresh in your memory, and you remember the witnesses and that th
as to Scott's lameness, all the witnesses that they had, all the wit
trained by More testify as to the lameness. We had a Miss Ameli
stand, and we also had a young lady by the name of Mary or Ros
glad she is not here to hear me mispronounce her name; it would nc
you will imagine. Now, gentlemen, I agree that she was bright;
was keen, but I don't agree that she was truthful, and when my Bro
his argument in commenting upon that witness, alluded to her in
your own daughters, I ask you if you were not mortified and asham
was, ready at repartee, and when I asked her certain questions she
her witty retort, and when yesterday I asked her in regard to some
gave me a flippant "none of your business," and when I inquired w

torted she did not choose to repeat. I agree she was self-assured and of ready wit, but where did she get it? She got it by chaffering with *men*! This woman who had been going around in one place a month, in another house three weeks, in another house four weeks, keeping house for a man three weeks, and at last placed in the arms of the mother-in-law of More, and stays there for a year, paying her and her mother's board, when her house rent is unpaid, her butchers' bills are unpaid, and her grocer's bill is unpaid, and she here glittering with jewelry and bedizened with elegant apparel! Mr. Foreman, to modify Watts a little, let me say that "The painted courtezan is known through the disguise they wear."

And then who was their champion, who was the witness who was their champion man, and who remembered dates; who remembered. the condition of his face, who remembered whether or not he had a full beard or a moustache, who it was that remembered about his lameness, who was able to recollect the fact because he was in his way when he was putting a new string in the piano? They called a man by the name of Decker, who by his own confession upon the stand, is a cheat and a swindler, and a knave, and that, too, in the meanest of all aspects. Cheating his own relations, and a perjurer by his own confession. Swearing here upon the stand that in his answer in the courts of justice, when he had been arraigned for fraud, and had sworn to facts, was inquired of whether he did not afterwards confess that the facts that he had sworn to were false, said, "only part of them." And that is a sample of their testimony. That shows the reservoir from which they draw, and which gives a complexion to all this testimony about an alibi, and I am willing to leave it just there. But, gentlemen, my learned Brother, in his remarks, suggested to us that, the case of the government was more remarkable for its suppressions than for what it had proved. I do not wonder that the thought occurred to my excellent friend, but that he should have been unwise enough to suggest it to you, certainly excited my surprise. They need never have had Decker. They need never have had Miss Ballou According to their own testimony here was the wife of Scott, who knew every fact, who knew all about the case, who knew where he was, what his business was, knew not only where he was on the 26th of January, but who knew where he was on the 7th of February, and where he was during all these times of which Edson testifies with such circumstantiality, and yet—there she sits!

Mr. Leonard—I don't think, your Honor, that what Mr. Gillett is saying is competent.

Judge Bacon—A wife, by law, is a competent witness; but if she refuses to be one, the government cannot compel her to be one.

Mr. Leonard—That matter has not been discussed, your Honor.

Mr. Gillett—Then I propose to discuss it.

My Brother Leonard opened the question. It has been opened that if the defendants saw fit, they could go upon the stand and testify, and my Brother Leonard gave the reasons fully to the jury why he did not place them in the witness box to testify in their own behalf, and I propose to reply to him. The whole question has been opened by the defense. In the last term of the court in Hampden County, Chief Justice Brigham so ruled. There is nothing that the defense shall allege in his case that the government cannot reply to legitimately.

Judge Bacon—I think the defense gave a reason why they did not call the defendants, and it may be discussed.

Mr. Leonard—The reason is simply a personal reason entirely. I only wish to have my rights here.

Judge Bacon—The counsel in his argument discusses the reason why the defendants and why the wife of one of the defendants is not called. I think the government have a right to comment upon these reasons, and upon what reasons they claim really exist.

Mr. Leonard—Your Honor will save me the point.

Mr. Gillett—My Brother Leonard says I cannot comment upon the wife's not testifying. As his Honor has just suggested, they cannot compel the wife to testify, but if she shall incline to testify for her husband, she can. But pray tell me if there is any such relationship, that she shall have any delicacy in testifying in behalf of Dunlap. And yet there she sat. Two honest German girls came to the stand, who make an important point in this case. My Brother Leonard inquires if they were

called in reply to anything. One of them had been here two or three
ing, of course, that they could not be so utterly desperate in their c
compelled to leave off Mrs. Scott, and the other only came here yeste
before for the purpose of rebutting that testimony, and here Mrs. Scot
these two girls swear, one of them that she went there on the 31st day
ing the time by the day that Mrs. Scott's sister left; she says fu
remained there a week and four days; that Scott was at home during
Saturday, the 5th day of February, when Scott left home, was not la
return until Wednesday night, the 9th. The 5th day of February w
went to Springfield. He came home again on Wednesday night. He
before the pressure of that German girl's hand. She swears to it, and
girl swears that she went there on Monday, the 7th, and that Scott w
and she did not see him until Thursday morning; that the other girl
house, and that he was not lame; and suddenly, on Friday, unexpecte
and Mr. Scott packed up their things and left the house and went to i
board, when, according to the testimony of Raphael, the agent
he had paid his rent up to the first of May next, a month and
that he gave up the rent of this house with its marble pillars, and yet
as my Brother Leonard states, that in the little domestic arrang
obliged to have his clothes mended by a tailor, to whom he present
cane! I say these two German girls go to the stand with this testim
presence of Mrs. Scott, and she is silent. But what is more signific
there, Dunlap there, Scott there, and listening to this conclusive, dam
and in consultation with their counsel, yet my skillful friends do not
to ask those girls a question! Not one question! Didn't dare, if t
call Scott and Dunlap and Mrs. Scott to the stand; didn't dare to ap
common tests that apply to all witnesses who speak falsely. And bo
not only swear that Scott wore a moustache, and in their ingenuous
cated way tell you that Mr. "Barton" was in good health, and th
Barton. And my Brother Leonard tries to explain to you why the c
not called upon the stand, and he says to you in explanation, that he
a defendant to the stand who was tried for a crime. Then, Mr. Fore
men, he never defended a man whom he believed to be innocent.
that, if an innocent man were defended, not only my Brother Leona
from the risk of putting an innocent man upon the stand, but could
nocent man off? If Scott and Dunlap were innocent, think you, in s
counsel, they would not have seized that witness stand and have
privilege of telling you their truthful story? My Brother Leonard
not believe them if they told their story. Why not? Why not? T
reason for not believing them, except that they are guilty. If the
could they not have told their story of innocence? Could not, at
man, could not Scott and Dunlap at least give us the history of one
one single hour, in all their lifetime, down to the period they were
jail, of any honest labor or employment anywhere or for anybody
Couldn't they have given us a little biography that should have let ir
on their mysterious lives? But instead of giving us anything, they
conjectures and to such facts as we can gather. And, gentlemen, th
of any labor that they have ever performed in their lifetime, and the
any work that they ever did in their lifetime, or any implements of
employed, are these burglars' tools found in their possession when the
This is the first evidence that we have from anybody suggesting any
did, excepting such as comes from Edson. Couldn't they have expla
And then, having been found with these tools, they go before the m
raigned and asked for their names; they withheld even their names, t
that silence is a part of their defence.

    Gentlemen, I do not propose to detain you any longer. We have
prove to you that these defendants are guilty. We have endeavored
the first place by the uncorroborated testimony of an accomplice; we
to you his testimony, which we say is the most extraordinary piece o
was ever given on a witness stand in the whole history of crimina

and we ask you to believe it from its internal evidence, from its intrinsic probability and the impossibility of the story being otherwise than true. Then we introduce evidence before you of certain corroborative facts, and we show to you that he is corroborated in various points; we show to you that he was corroborated by the Wilkesbarre affair, by the affair at Syracuse, that he was corroborated by the interview between Connors and Williams, made in accordance with the agreement previously made between the parties; and also from the fact that Scott went to Springfield and Connors went after him, and that he came back in consequence of what Edson himself had achieved in that direction. Then we went with you to the scene of the burglary, the dwelling-house of Whittelsey, and I ask you to consider the evidence derived from the witnesses there, Mr. Whittelsey, Mrs. Whittelsey and Mrs. Page; and then we ask you to rely upon the testimony of Mr. Crafts, Mr. Mantor, and Mrs. Crafts; then we ask you to go to Springfield, and to rely upon the testimony which we gathered there, and we have grouped this testimony together, making out, as we believe, conclusively and inextricably, the guilt of the defendants. In their endeavors to explain the testimony which has been introduced by the defense, and we claim that that testimony, instead of going one single step towards their acquittal, only involves them more and more in the confusion of guilt.

Now, gentlemen, I leave the further consideration of this important cause. The question for you to decide is, are the defendants guilty, or are they innocent, upon the evidence? The eloquent appeal made by my learned friend to you, in regard to the practical result that must follow a conviction, should not influence your honest minds. Whether they are to see again the light of the sun, or the moon, or the stars, is not one of the consequences that you can be made responsible for. Such appeals are not appropriate to this tribunal; they may be pertinent elsewhere.

The diversified functions of our government are wisely distributed, and the duties of its various departments do not clash. The cloud of justice which settles down upon this tribunal, is armed with executing thunders. Only as it encircles the brow of the executive does it reveal its silver lining of mercy. Remember, gentlemen, that mercy to criminals is cruelty to the innocent. I trust your verdict may not be such a one as shall create a gala-day among the thirty-five thousand professional thieves of the city of New York, and especially among the aristocracy in villainy, to which I claim that the defendants belong, who make that city the base of their operations, and the whole country the theater of their achievements; and these banded miscreants shall not exult, that at last Massachusetts has become a safe field for their professional experiments, and of all places, and the last place, that the old County of Hampshire has at length opened her door of invitation to masked burglars and midnight robbers. God forbid! Rather let your verdict prove a terror to evil doers, and a joy to those who do well. Let us reassure the people of this Commonwealth, as to-day our ears are stunned by the echoes of lawless violence in other States, that here, if nowhere else, her citizens shall be protected in their property, and their lives, by night as well as by day, and especially in the sanctuary of their own homes, the place "where we all live, or bear no life," so that when the day of honest toil is done, and the darkness comes on, and "God giveth his beloved sleep," the solitary, even, whom "He hath established in families," may rest in their beds in peace, and in conscious security, beneath the silent omnipresence of the law.

The Jury Return a Verdict of Guilty.

Judge Bacon charged the jury, and at about three o'clock they retired to deliberate upon their verdict. At about six, they reported to the court that they had agreed upon a verdict of *Guilty*. At first, the jury stood ten for conviction and two for acquittal, and the two yielded after the points upon which they at first doubted had been discussed. They were at no time very strenuous, but were a little in doubt. The announcement of the verdict made a profound sensation in the court-room, but apparently it made little impression upon the prisoners.

Exceptions Taken.—A New Trial Asked For.

The counsel for the defense took numerous exceptions to the rulings of the Judge during the two trials: one of the chief of which is the exception to the displacement of a juror from the panel by a challenge from the government after he had been accepted and sworn. The exceptions taken during the la t trial will be filed with the Clerk of the Courts on or before August 2. Then they will be examined by the counsel for the prosecution, and if they are found to be in accordance with the facts of the case, they will be reported to the Supreme Court, in September. If they are not found to be correct, then the presiding Judge will be called in to assist in shaping them. Arguments will be heard upon them pro and con in September, and if the exceptions are sustained, the c se will be put on the list for trial again in December; if they are overruled, the defendants will be called up in December for sentence.

[From the New York Sunday Sun, July 29.—Written by E. J. Edwards, Special Reporter.]

Gigantic Bank Robberies.

A Remarkable Series of Crimes—Edson the Lock Expert—His Connection with Connors, Scott, and Dunlap.—Nearly $3,000,000 taken from So-called Burglar Proof Safes.

The old-time bank burglar went out of the business when scientific men invented the combination lock. Bank men and safe men imagined that at last something had been found that was burglar-proof. But in 1872 a robbery in Louisville opened their eyes, and this was followed for a period of four years by a series of robberies and attempts which not only had never been equaled, so far as daring and success were concerned, but which showed that burglars of ability had got the best of combination locks.

From the similarity of method in all these robberies and attempts, it was plain that the same men were doing them; but they covered their tracks so skilfully, that, although some of them were suspected, no proof was ever obtained of their guilt, excepting in the case of one man, until the remarkable developments which followed the arrest of Scott, Dunlap and Connors for robbing the Northampton National Bank.

Now, that Scott and Dunlap are convicted, and will probably spend the rest of their days in State prison, the whole story of the organization of this Ring, of their various attempts and of their successful robbery of nearly three millions of money and bonds in the four years that they operated together, may be told for the first time.

Robert C. Scott spent his boyhood in the town of Warsaw, Ill. He had served one term in the Illinois penitentiary for grand larceny, and was serving a second for stabbing a man, when he met in the penitentiary an old bank robber, Tom Riley, alias Tom Scott, alias Scarfaced Tom. When both were released, Scott was introduced by Riley, who is now in Auburn, to James Dunlap, who is either a Scotchman or of Scotch descent. Both Scott and Dunlap were men of strength, health, nerve, patience, and brains. How soon after they met Billy Connors, so well known in New York, was taken into the Ring, is not known, but it is certain that within a few months after their acquaintanceship, the Falls City Bank of Louisville, Ky., was broken into and robbed by the Ring, and some $200,000 stolen. This was in 1872, and was the first bank robbed by the Ring. Less is known about the means employed in robbing this bank than of those that followed. But soon after this robbery, the partners began to scour through the country, looking for weak banks. Some of them, probably Connors, "spotted" the Second National Bank of Elmira, and, after a thorough investigation, found that the only way that they could work was through the floor of the Young Men's Christian Association room, which was directly over the vault of the bank. But a difficulty presented itself. The door of the room was an iron one, and locked with a Hall lock. It was necessary to be able to open this lock in some way every night in order to work at the vault, and they did not know how a Hall lock could be opened, nor could they learn.

LOCK SECRETS.

They decided that in some way they must get the secret of the Hall lock. Connors spent a great deal of time, and at last heard that a salesman of Herring's safes stabled a horse at Ryan's, in Thirty-fourth street. Ryan had been crooked years before, and to him Connors went, and Ryan consented to bring this salesman, Edson, and Connors, together. Ryan began by hinting to Edson that he had splendid opportunities to make money easily and safely,

and so, gradually leading the way, he at last asked Edson to be allowed to introduce a friend to him. This friend was Billy Connors, and at the first interview nothing more than very gentle hints passed. Some six interviews were had, and at the last, which took place in a saloon in Prince street, near Broadway, Edson consented for $50,000 to tell Connors how a Hall lock could be opened. Connors went away in great glee, and told the rest of the Ring that he had got a man now who could open any lock in the country for them. Then the plan was arranged. Connors got some one in Elmira to send a letter to Herring & Co., inquiring about safes, and, as was expected, Edson was sent to see about it. He went to Elmira, stopping at the Rathbone House, and on the Sunday after his arrival a man came in and sat opposite to him at dinner. This man asked Edson whether his name was Edson, and being told that it was, said he had a letter of introduction. This man was Robert C. Scott. It was agreed that Scott should put a paper wad into the Hall lock that night, so that it would not work the next morning. Meanwhile, Edson was to let it be known that he was in town, and it was expected that, naturally, he would be called on to repair the lock. It happened just as was expected, and while Edson repaired the lock he got an impression of the key, which he gave Scott, and the difficulty of approach to the bank vaults was then cleared away.

The burglars, before they found Edson, went so far as to break into the house of the Secretary of the Y. M. C. A., and to feel in his pockets for the keys, simply to get an impression of them. But the Secretary had hidden the keys under the carpet, and they were foiled. This Secretary was greatly surprised the next morning to see traces of burglary, and to find that nothing had been taken, and he never understood it.

SHAM HOUSEKEEPING.

After the key was finally obtained, arrangements were made. A woman who lived in Baltimore was hired to go to Elmira and take a house somewhere in the suburbs. She was represented as the wife of a man who was away a great deal. This house was simply furnished with cooking utensils, a few blankets, and a set of window curtains throughout. This woman made a great display of keeping house, sweeping the steps and yard every day with great vigor. Here Scott, Dunlap, Red Leary, Billy Connors and John Berry spent their days, going out at night only, and they were never seen. They lived there six weeks. Every night they went to the Y. M. C. A. room, unlocked the door, took up the flooring, and went to work. They removed ton after ton of stones and carried them up to the top of the Opera House building in baskets. There were four feet of solid masonry to be dug through, some of the stones weighing a ton ; then a layer of railroad iron and a plate of 1½ inch steel. They got through all of this but the last plate ; but one night President Pratt, of the bank, having occasion to go into the vault, saw a layer of white dust on the floor. He suspected something, and got an officer. An alarm was given to the gang, and all got away but Berry. He was arrested at the door, and is now serving a sentence in Auburn prison, his time being up next September, for this attempted burglary. Afterward the air pump which they expected to use to blow powder into the safe, was found in the lumber yard, where they had hidden it. Connors the same night was seized by a man at the depot, but he wrenched himself away, and walked to Watkins, N. Y., and from there took a boat to Geneva, and met Scott and Dunlap on the New York Central train, they having gone from Elmira to Buffalo, and then taken the train to New York. They had expected to get some $200,000 in greenbacks and $6 - 000,000 in bonds.

After helping Berry on his trial and se-ing that his family was taken care of, they agreed to scout again. Dunlap went West, and after some time in February, 1874, sent to Scott to make up a party, and bring the air pump, as he had "found something to go to work at." Scott made up the party, which consisted of himself, Tom Draper, Dave Cummings, alias Little Dave, Tom Bigelow, Billy Flynn, and George Mason, and they, going by different routes, met Dunlap in Quincy, Ill. Here the Baltimore woman had hired a house, and in it the gang lived. and from it went to work. Getting access to the room over the vault, they took up the flooring every night, and at last got down to the safes upon which they expected to use the air pump. But, for one reason or another, they had to wait two weeks for a good night to consummate the job. At last the night came, and Scott and Dunlap, after taking off the brick top, went down into the vault. Then the seams of the upper safe were all puttied up, excepting a little hole at the top and bottom. On a piece of paper was placed fine powder, and held to the little hole at the top of the vault, and the air pump was applied to the lower hole ; and thus the powder was sucked in. Then a little pistol was attached to the upper hole, loaded only with powder, a string attached to the trigger, and at a safe distance discharged ; but there was only a puff. Another attempt was more successful, and $120,- 000 in money and some $700,000 in bonds were taken. The bank acknowledged a loss of only $80,000. Neither the money nor the bonds have been recovered.

SUMPTUOUS LIVING.

The party returned to New York, and for a time lived in great style. The choicest wines and cigars, fast horses and women melted their money. It was at this time that Scott bought the celebrated trotter Knox which made a sensation on the Coney Island road. Many persons will now learn with amazement that the dashing young man who cut such a swath in the summer of 1874 speeding his splendid horse down the Coney Island road, was Robert C. Scott, the burglar, and that the blonde moustached man with him, who seemed such a jolly good fellow, was his pal and companion now in Northampton jail, James Dunlap.

In the fall of 1874 their money gave out again, and they began to look around for a fresh job. Edson had nothing to do with the Quincy robbery, and the Ring had not seen him for nearly a year. As the air pump was Edson's they paid him for its use in the Quincy robbery, but only about half the amount they had promised to pay. In the fall, however, Dunlap went to see him. Edson then told Dunlap that he wished to sever all connection with them, but said Dunlap, "Berry, who is now in Auburn, wants to squeal, and I am the only one who can stop him. Would you want your family to know of the disgrace and your employers ?" With this threat held over him, Edson consented to go and examine the Saratoga National Bank, which he did ; but he reported to them that the attempt would not be feasible. Then they "spotted" the Long Island Savings Bank, and this appeared very "good ground," because they could hire the adjoining premises. But they had some difficulty in getting any one to hire these premises. They had been piping the Atlantic Bank in Brooklyn, but had given it up for the Long Island. Connors was sent West to find a man who would hire the premises, but he could not get any one. Finally, Billy Maher, a partner of Max Shinburn, the famous burglar, was given $100 to hire the adjoining premises ; but he "jumped away" with the money. Just at this

time, a Jew had come from the vicinity of Des Moines, Iowa, to New York, to get some one to go out there and rob the county treasury. Scott and George Mason went out with this Jew, took the job, and this caused the first trouble in the Ring, Dunlap feeling very hard toward Scott. The Des Moines job failed, having been given away, and Scott and Mason escaped arrest by jumping from a railroad train, leaving all their tools. They walked some twenty miles in a freezing ice storm, and their legs were badly cut up and bruised by their frequent falls on the ice.

BUSINESS AND PLEASURE.

Before the attempt upon the Long Island Bank, they had intended to rob the bank on Nantucket Island. Scott, Dunlap and " Red " Leary had visited the island while on a pleasure trip, and found the bank an easy one to get at. They found an old sea captain in New York who agreed to pilot them to Nantucket and back for a share in the spoils. They left New York in a sloop, and sailed through the Sound. When off Block Island, a fearful storm came up. Every man in the party, except the captain, was fearfully sea-sick, and none of them knew one rope from another. They expected to go to the bottom, but finally they reached Greenport, Long Island, where they left the captain to take care of himself and vessel.

After a while it was learned that the First National Bank of Covington, Ky., had a great deal of money in its vaults, and was a good one to "work." Scott, Connors, Red Leary, Jim Draper and others went to Covington, but Dunlap was not included in the party on account of his quarrel with Scott. The vault of this bank is under the Opera House door. The gang went in every night, removed the orchestra seats, took up the floor, and easily took off the top of the vault. When all was ready Connors stayed outside to watch. Scott and Leary went down into the vault, and charged the safe with powder. The explosion was a terrific one, as a little nitro-glycerine was used. The ceiling of the bank fell, and there was a big shower of bricks, dust, and mortar. The noise was so loud that Connors was frightened. He gave an alarm, and the gang fled, leaving behind $400,000 in greenbacks and $1,500,000 in good bonds. The alarm was needless, as no one went to the bank until 8 o'clock next day. Connors was blamed for giving a false alarm and thus losing such a rich haul, and it was said by all that had Dunlap been there he would not have gone without the money. The first thing to do, they agreed, was to get Dunlap back into the party.

The Rockville, Conn., Bank was next pitched upon. Before deciding to try this bank, they examined banks at Plymouth, Bloomsburg, and Wilkesbarre, Pa., and at Syracuse, N. Y.; but some one told Dunlap that the Rockville Bank was an easy one to get into. Scott went to Rockville in his assumed character of horse dealer, and Dunlap and Connors followed soon afterward. They had no trouble in getting into the room over the bank, and on the first night found that there were only a few layers of brick between the top of the vault and the inside. They worked upon this top about a week, taking out a few bricks every night. One night Dunlap warned Scott that they had got to work very carefully ; if they did not, the top would give way. The night before they expected to get access to the vault, Scott was jamming at the bricks with a jimmy, By accident he forced it through the top of the vault, and it fell inside. As there was no way to get it out, and as its discovery would lead to a careful guarding of the bank they gave up the job, and rode to Hartford, and then to New York.

ENTERING A BANK THROUGH THE ROOF.

The Ring were now getting very short of money, and decided to make another attempt on the easiest bank. They at first thought of taking the bank at Bloomsburg, Pa., but Connors, who had been to Pittston, came back and reported that the Pittston Bank was "good ground." The party was made up, and about the last of October, 1875, they began operations. The First National Bank of Pittston is, or was then, a one-story building, covered with a tin roof. After some consultation it was decided that work had better be begun on the roof. Dunlap got some red putty in New York; some of the tin roofing was taken up, and then the boards of the roof were removed. This work took one night. The boards were carefully put back, the tin put down and joined with red putty. So carefully was this done that, although there was a hard rain and sleet storm the next day, the roof did not leak a drop. The next night the tin and boards were removed again, and work was begun on the top of the vault. A layer of bricks was removed and the roof put back. This work was carried on until only one layer of bricks remained. This was removed on the night of the burglary, Nov. 4, 1875. The top of the vault was taken off in two hours' time, and then Scott and Dunlap let themselves down into the vault. Connors piped outside and the others were placed where they were needed. In the vault were three Marvin spherical safes. There was also a burglar alarm in the vault. This troubled Scott and Dunlap. They at length decided to surround it with boards. Then they called for the air pump, the dynamite and the powder, which were let down to them. Scott applied the air pump to one of the safes, but they overcharged it with powder and it blew half the door off. Then they opened it by inserting dynamite and exploding it. In the safe they found $500 in currency and $60,000 in good bonds. Next they attacked another safe. They first broke off the spindle, and, inserting a little dynamite, blew off a plate. Then they inserted another charge of dynamite, and another, blowing off plate after plate. They had only one more plate to blow off when they heard Connors giving the alarm. In this safe was a very large sum of money. While they were in the vault, Scott and Dunlap caused twelve explosions, one of them a terrific one; but they did not dare waste time by leaving the vault before an explosion and then returning, so they remained in the vault throughout, and trusted to the boards they had put around the burglar alarm to protect them. Just after the last explosion Connors saw a man looking out of a window of a house near by, and it was for this that he gave the alarm. It appears that, of the twelve explosions, the man heard the last two, and went out to see what the noise was caused by.

When Scott and Dunlap came out of this vault they were almost exhausted. Their clothes were wringing wet, although it was a cold night, and their lungs were filled with the noxious and disagreeable gas which an explosion of dynamite makes. They could hardly walk at first, and had to be stimulated. Then they walked to Leigh, some thirty miles, and, taking an early train, were in New York the next afternoon. The bonds were afterward "compromised" back to the bank through the aid of New York lawyers, but the amount obtained was so small that it was decided to do another job as soon as possible.

A TREMENDOUS JOB.

In the summer before these two last attempts, George Miles, the Barre bank robber, told Scott that there was a bank in Northampton, Mass., that could be beaten. They had gone to Northampton several times, and had sent Edson there before the Pittston robbery. But they found difficulties, and Connors was doubtful of their success. These were the night watchman, the four keys in different hands, the combination, which was divided between two persons. They decided that it would be useless to try to dig into the vault; if Edson could get impressions of the four keys, and could get the combination into one person's keeping, they could do the rest. Edson did his part, as the reports printed in the papers have shown. He got impressions of the four keys, and by his advice the bank gave the entire combination to Mr. Whittelsey, the Cashier. After talking over many plans, they decided to take a bolder step than they had yet taken —to force the combination from Mr. Whittelsey at

the point of the pistol, then jump suddenly upon and overpower the night policemen, gag them, take them to the lockup, and lock them in with the prisoners. But Dunlap accidentally learned that the night watchman went off duty at 4 o'clock in the morning, and as that would give them nearly three hours of darkness at that time of the year, they decided to spend the night between midnight and 4 o'clock at Whittelsey's house. How they did their work is now well known. The bonds and papers were taken away in pillowcases, and hidden in one of the vaults in the Northampton burying-ground, whence they were removed some time in February.

When the burglars found out that they had obtained a million and a quarter of money and bonds, they were almost beside themselves with joy. They estimated that on a compromise they would clear between three and four hundred thousand dollars, and they were certain that the bank and individual losers would be so anxious to get the "stuff" back that the burglars would be safe, even if it was suspected that they did the job. Of this last they had little fear. They had done so many jobs, and left no traces behind, and were so confident that they had left none in this case, that they felt no anxiety, and began steps at once for a compromise. Then the quarrel broke out. Edson began to negotiate with the bank people, and saw very soon that they suspected him of having had something to do with the burglary. Meanwhile, the bank had put the business into the hands of Pinkerton's agency, by which all the operations of the gang were afterwards ferreted out.

EDSON REVEALS ALL.

Several interviews were had by Edson and the bank officers, and, through Edson, Connors and Mr. Williams, one of the bank officers, were brought together. But these negotiations all failed, and Edson saw that he was falling between two stools. Meanwhile, Pinkerton's men had suspected Scott and Dunlap, and one of their detectives was constantly shadowing them. At last Edson told Mr. Williams in an interview : "I am trying to effect a negotiation, but I am left by these men in a very bad light by their constant playing with you and me, after you take the trouble to come to New York. Now, sir, if you don't reach a settlement, at the next meeting, by G—d, I will tell you who the men are."

The negotiation fell through, and Edson kept his word. Going to Pinkerton's office by request of the bank, he gave a detailed history of the robbery, which led to the arrest of Scott, Dunlap and Connors and to the flight of Red Leary. When Connors escaped from Ludlow street jail, the control of the securities was given to him, and he has furnished some of the money for the defence of these men.

Scott, who was a skilful organizer and planner, was the leader of the Ring, but the execution of the dangerous work was always put into Dunlap's hands. Dunlap has been often arrested, but has invariably managed in one way or another to get out of his difficulties, and he fancied that his luck would not desert him now. Connors generally "piped"—that is, watched outside—during a robbery, and was expected to conduct negotiations for the return of the securities. The rest of the gang were simply assistants. It is known that some of these last have long been dissatisfied with the treatment received from Scott and Dunlap, and are pleased that the leaders have got into trouble. In fact, Edson, before he betrayed the gang, received a letter from one of these dissatisfied men, warning him to look out "that he did not get tarred with the same stick that he was at Quincy" —referring to the attempt of Scott, Dunlap, and Connors to cheat him out of his fair proportion of the spoils of the Quincy robbery.

The amount stolen by this gang in four years is nearly three millions of dollars in money and securities, most of which has not been recovered.

THE NORTHAMPTON BANK ROBBERY

Reviewed in the Light of Recent Revelations.

People who took any special interest in the great Northampton bank robbery have had frequent occasion to note that on the return of the anniversary of that event some fresh and highly entertaining revelation was sure to be brought out concerning it. And some of them who were in the bloom of youth on the morning of January 27, 1876, when the startling truth that Cashier Whittelsey and his household had been tied and gagged and a round $1,500,000 in securities carried away in bags from the Old bank electrified this valley and the world, have begun to feel that they shall never live to bear the last of that robbery. Not to review the different sensations which the seven revolving years have brought, it seems that the recent suit against the bank by Mrs Fanny D. Wylie, to recover $40,000 in bonds which she had deposited with them for safe-keeping at the time of the robbery, tried in the New York courts and won by the defendant, brought out considerable of the true inwardness of the whole affair, hitherto known only to those inside the directors' ring.

For a year after the robbery the bank tried to make negotiations for the return of the steal, but the burglars wanted at the outset to retain 75 per cent of the whole, and neither side could ever get within $100,000 of the other's ideas. Then the bank, advised by Pinkerton, undertook to arrest as many of the theives as they could. They got Scott and Dunlap, as everybody knows, and secured 20 years for them at Concord. They also arrested "Red" Leary, "Shang" Draper and Billy Connors, but they didn't keep them, as everybody knows. After Scott and Dunlap had been shut up some little time they sent word to the bank that they could cause the return of all that had been stolen except the government bonds and $100,000 in other securities. Although they were confined apart from each other they both told the bank men that Dunlap controlled the funds, and that he would surrender them in return for a pardon or new trial for each of them. It was also known that the $40,000 in government bonds and the $13,000 cash were divided immediately after the robbery, and that only a few days before Scott and Dunlap were arrested $100,000 in the most available securities had been set aside to be turned into money for the help of any of the gang who might be arrested. The $25,000 in bonds which Director Hinckley recovered by paying $6000 belonged to this lot, as did the $10,000 for which Mrs Wylie has just sued in vain. Knowing these things, the bank men, according to statements recently published

in the New York Sun, undertook to ▮▮▮▮ ec the different governors of Massachusetts ▮de something for Scott and Dunlap. It wa▮ ▮▮, however, Gov Long remarking that whe▮ ▮▮y showed any signs of penitence and ▮ ▮l done what they could by way of restoring the property, it would be ample time to consider appeals for executive clemency. Meanwhile both men tried to escape on the same day, having probably been able to communicate with each other and their associates out of prison through the friends who were allowed by law to see each of them, for an attempt was made from outside to help them. For three years and a half they stuck to the story that Dunlap controlled the bulk of the steal.

Then Scott was attacked with quick consumption, and his mother, who came on from Illinois to see him, urged him to make restitution. He agreed to do it, and so did Dunlap, who confessed that "Red" Leary was the man in charge of the funds, and that the latter had written him that they should be given up, so that Scott might die out of prison and his own term be shortened, but that Leary had apparently changed his mind. Leary, who had escaped from Ludlow-street jail and been to Europe and returned, was in due time arrested near New York on a clew given by Dunlap, and taken to Northampton jail. Then, for the first time, Scott and Dunlap were allowed to have an interview in Concord prison. During the three hours they were together, in the presence of a keeper, they wrote a letter to Leary claiming the right to have two-sevenths of what he held delivered to the bank, under the old agreement that the seven burglars should share alike, and threatening to appear at Northampton and "down" him if he did not follow out their suggestion; also promising not to harm him if he did. Leary took three weeks to consider the matter, and during that time it is supposed that he secured the consent of all the thieves interested in the surrender. Then word came to the bank officers that a New York lawyer would tell them where the securities could be found, and the full amount of the robbery was subsequently recovered from a safe deposit company in that city—minus the $152,000 in government bonds, cash and a reserve mutual aid fund, referred to above. It is thought that Leary alone knew where the property was hid and that he revealed the place by means of a diagram which he drew up in prison and sent down to New York. The securities were in good condition when they were returned, having apparently been protected in their hiding-place by oiled silk and other wrappings.

The rest of the story is soon told. Scott and Dunlap did not appear against Leary, and he was discharged, together with Draper and Connors. Scott died in prison soon after, and Dunlap is still working out his 20 years' term. Leary and Draper are New York saloon-keepers, and Connors calls himself a sporting man. Brady, another of the seven, is in the Clinton, New York, prison for robbery. Greer never was arrested and the seventh man is unknown. Pinkerton thinks that if Leary and Connors had not been allowed to escape from the Ludlow-street jail the $100,000 reserve fund might all have been recovered. He says that he has never known any other bank to show so much perseverance in following up burglars. The cost of this battle is estimated at $30,000.